MAN'S WORST FRIEND

Frank unlatched the crate lid, lifted it off, and stumbled backward as a large, friendly German shepherd bounded out and licked his face.

"I think he likes you," Joe said. "I wonder what his name is."

Frank studied the dog's collar. "He's got some kind of tag. Maybe his name's on it." The German shepherd sat obediently as Frank parted its fur and grasped a flat metal disk attached to its collar. A faint, high-pitched whine sounded in Frank's ear. "What's that noise?" he said.

"I don't hear anything," Joe replied.

Frank suddenly became aware of another, more disturbing noise. The dog let out a low, mean growl and its lips curled back in a vicious snarl—just before it lunged for Frank's throat.

**Books in THE HARDY BOYS
CASEFILES™ Series**

THE HARDY BOYS CASEFILES NO. 69

MAYHEM IN MOTION

FRANKLIN W. DIXON

AN ARCHWAY PAPERBACK
Published by SIMON & SCHUSTER
New York   London   Toronto   Sydney   Tokyo   Singapore

An Archway paperback first published
in Great Britain by Simon & Schuster in 1995
A Viacom Company

Simon & Schuster Ltd
West Garden Place
Kendal Street
London W2 2AQ

Simon & Schuster of Australia Pty Ltd
Sydney

A CIP catalogue record for this book
is available from the British Library.

ISBN 0-671-85177-2
Printed and bound in Great Britain by
HarperCollins*Manufacturing*, Glasgow

Chapter

1

"YOUR TIME IS UP," Joe Hardy muttered under his breath as the minute hand on the wall clock moved up to the twelve.

Of course the history teacher paid no attention to the clock and kept on talking until the shrill clanging of the bell cut him off. Joe absently ran his hand through his short blond hair, heaved his six-foot frame out of the cramped school desk, and headed out of the classroom. After a quick stop at his locker to grab his coat, he joined the other Bayport High students swarming toward the exit and freedom.

His brother, Frank, was waiting for him on the outside steps that led to the student parking lot. "What took you so long?" Frank asked with a grin, the late-afternoon sunlight bright in his intense brown eyes.

"This is a switch," Joe said. "Usually I have to wait for you."

"We had a chemistry test," Frank explained. "I finished early, and the teacher let me take off."

"That figures," Joe grumbled. "You're the only person I know who thinks chemistry is easy—and fun."

Frank's grin widened. "Look on the bright side. At least I waited for you."

Joe stuck his hand in his coat pocket and fished out a set of car keys. "That's because I have these," he responded, dangling the keys in his brother's face.

Frank pulled out a matching set of keys. "Wrong again, boy genius. I waited for you because I always wait for you. I've been doing it for seventeen years."

Joe chuckled, and his breath turned to a puff of steam in the crisp winter air. He stopped laughing suddenly and grabbed his brother's arm. "Who's that?" he asked in a loud whisper, pointing at a tall, slim girl moving across the parking lot in long, smooth strides. She was wearing blue jeans and a short, flame red down parka. Her ash blond hair hung halfway down her back and fluttered in the breeze as she walked.

Frank shrugged. "I've never seen her before. She must be new."

2

"Maybe she could use a couple of friends to show her around town," Joe said.

"Maybe she could use a little help with her car," Frank replied as he watched the girl stop next to a compact sedan the same color as her parka. The left front tire was flat, and she was crouching down now to look at it.

"Let's give her a hand with the spare," Joe said, and he set off at a jog.

Frank followed at a less urgent pace. He knew one spare tire would be useless. He had noticed something his brother had missed. Both tires on the left side were flat. As he got closer he could see the gaping slashes where the tires had been ripped open with a knife. He walked around the car and saw a mirror image of the scene on the other side. All four tires had been slashed.

The girl stood up and faced Joe. Her eyes were almost level with his. Joe couldn't tell exactly what color they were. One moment they were gray, and the next they were a hazy blue. "Nice town you've got here," she said. "I was safer in Manhattan." Her tone was casual—but Joe could tell she was rattled. Her defenses were up, and she wasn't going to show weakness to a couple of strangers.

"I was going to say 'Welcome to Bayport,' " Joe remarked as he caught sight of the gouged rear tire. "But something tells me that would be a mistake. We've got a phone in our van. You can use it to call a tow truck."

"That sounds like a pickup line," she said

3

with a faint smile. "How do I know you didn't slash my tires to entice me into your truck?"

"It's not a truck," Joe said defensively. "It's a van."

The girl laughed softly. "Oh, then I guess it's all right. Before I use your phone, though, I have an important question."

"Fire away," Joe said.

"Who *are* you guys?"

Joe grinned and stuck out his right hand. "I'm Joe Hardy—and the guy searching for fingerprints on your tires is my brother, Frank."

"I'm Vanessa Bender," she said as they shook hands. She peered down at her ruined tires and frowned. "Does this sort of thing happen often around here?"

"Not really," Frank answered. "Bayport's a pretty quiet town. This doesn't look like some random vandalism job either. All four tires are slashed. I'd say somebody doesn't like you very much."

"I don't know anybody in Bayport," Vanessa responded. "We just moved here last week."

"Maybe they got the wrong car," Joe suggested.

"That's probably it," Vanessa said. She shivered slightly. "It's still creepy, though."

Joe shoved his hands in his coat pockets. "It's also cold. Let's get in the van, turn on the heater, and make that call."

Joe kept an eye out for the tow truck while they waited in the van. When the truck pulled into the parking lot, Joe and Vanessa got out

4

and waved the truck over to Vanessa's car. The driver scratched his head, saying, "I'll have to go back to the station and get a special rig for this. You didn't tell me it had four flats."

"How long will that take?" Vanessa asked.

"Not long to get the rig," the driver said. "But we won't be able to put new tires on before tomorrow afternoon."

"Just my luck," Vanessa said with a sigh. "I don't suppose there's a cabstand around here. It's a long walk home."

Joe bowed slightly and motioned toward the van. "Hardy taxi-van at your service. Reasonable rates and free in-flight entertainment."

Vanessa smiled. "Remind me to thank whoever slashed my tires. I might not have met you otherwise."

The late-afternoon sun hung low in the sky, shining right in Joe's eyes as he drove west, following Vanessa's directions. "Are you sure you know where we're going?" he asked doubtfully as they passed the city limits.

"Absolutely," Vanessa assured him. "Turn left at the next street. There's a viaduct that goes under the railroad tracks. On the other side you'll be able to see our house."

Vanessa's house turned out to be on a rambling old farm with a long gravel driveway. Frank's eyes moved over the snow-covered fields past the big, two-story farmhouse, and stopped at a bright red barn with four or five

5

cars parked in front. The building had been reno-
vated and painted recently. Skylights dotted the
roof, and Frank suspected that he wouldn't find
cows inside if he peered through one of the large
plate-glass windows on the ground floor.

"You don't see many barns with windows like
that," he remarked.

"You don't see many farms with this many
cars," Joe added. He found a spot to park the
van next to the house, and they got out. "Is
your father a car collector or something?"

"My father died when I was a baby," Vanessa
said. "I don't remember him at all. My mom
bought this place about six months ago. We
didn't move in until the studio was ready."

"Is your mother some kind of artist?" Joe
asked.

Vanessa smiled. "You might say that." She
took his hand and started to walk toward the
barn. "Come on. I'll show you."

Frank followed along behind them. Something
had clicked between Joe and Vanessa, and he
didn't want to crowd them. Frank had a steady
girlfriend, Callie Shaw. She was somewhere in
New Hampshire working on a video project for
school and wouldn't be back for a week.

The inside of the barn didn't look anything
like the inside of a barn. Frank felt as if he'd
been let loose in an electronic candy store. Most
of the space had been left open as a single, huge
room. It was filled with computers and video
equipment. Electrical cables snaked across the

linoleum floor and were held in place by thick strips of shiny silver tape. A man and two women were crowded around one of the computer terminals, staring intently at the screen.

"Hey, Mom!" Vanessa called out. "Look what followed me home from school!"

One of the women turned around. Frank thought she looked like an older, slightly shorter version of Vanessa. Her working clothes were definitely casual—an old, paint-stained sweatshirt and baggy gray slacks with big side pockets. She glanced at both of the Hardys before her gaze settled on Joe. Vanessa was still holding his hand.

"Well, you can't keep both of them," the woman said in a droll voice. "The food bills would bankrupt me before this project does."

"What kind of talk is that, Andrea?" another voice demanded. Frank stared at the second woman, who had been so interested in the computer monitor a few seconds earlier. "Rex Rover is going to be the most popular dog on television. We're going to be millionaires."

Joe turned to Vanessa. "Rex Rover?"

"An interstellar traveler who just happens to look like a dog," Vanessa managed to say with a straight face. "His spaceship crash-landed on earth."

Joe wasn't sure if he should laugh or call a mental hospital. He decided to play along. "How could he work the controls with his paws?"

7

"Apparently not very well," Vanessa said. "He crashed, didn't he?"

"Everybody knows that all animated characters have at least three fingers and an opposable thumb," the second woman responded.

"Animated?" Joe said. "You mean cartoons?"

"That's right," Vanessa's mother said. She gestured around the room. "All this high-tech hardware is wired up to make cartoon critters chase one another around your television set." She paused and gave her daughter a look that Joe had seen more than once in his own mother's eyes. "Do your new friends have names, Vanessa?"

"Oh, sure," Vanessa said, dropping Joe's hand. "Mom, this is Joe Hardy and his brother, Frank. Guys, this is my mother, the soon-to-be-famous Andrea Bender, president and founder of Animaniacs, Limited."

"You use all these computers for animation?" Frank asked.

Andrea nodded. "That's what's going to make me famous—or out of work. Traditional animation is mostly done by hand. At twenty-four frames a second and four layers of animation per frame, that's about six thousand drawings a minute. So it takes a lot of hands to make a half-hour cartoon show."

"Unless you computerize the whole operation," Frank ventured.

"Other companies have used computer animation, but not to the extent we do. Our new animation processes make it all possible,'' Andrea explained. ''With just a small staff and a handful of freelance artists, we're doing all the production for a brand-new animated television series. Of course, all these electronic gizmos are worthless without a good story to back them up.'' She gestured to the woman who had spoken earlier and the man standing next to her. ''Meet the creative team who dreamed up 'Rex Rover,' Skip Guzman and Lynn St. Pierre.''

Joe didn't think the pair could be any kind of team. In fact, they seemed to be a couple of cartoon characters themselves. The woman was tall enough to play professional basketball, and her blazing red hair stood out like some kind of warning flag. The man, on the other hand, had hardly any hair at all, and Joe doubted he could hold his head above water in the shallow end of a pool.

The man gave a curt nod and turned to Vanessa's mother. ''We'd better get back to work if you want that rewrite before I leave tonight.''

Frank glanced at his watch. ''We'd better get going, Joe. We have some errands to run for Dad before dinner.''

''My brother's right,'' Joe said to Vanessa. ''Our father's a private investigator. If we don't show up on time for dinner, he puts on his trenchcoat and starts interrogating all our friends.'' He was trying to sound cool but was sure he sounded like a complete nerd. He decided to keep talking, anyway. "How are you going to get to school tomorrow without a car?"

Vanessa smiled brightly. "I was dreading the bus. Could you pick me up at quarter to eight?"

The next morning Joe steered the van toward the railroad viaduct at seven forty-five on the dot. He had to wait while a large truck coming from the other direction rumbled through the underpass.

"A fire truck," Frank noted as the lime green hook-and-ladder truck rattled past. "It must be heading back to the station. I wonder where the fire was."

"How do you know it's not on its way *to* the fire?" Joe asked.

"The lights and siren weren't on," Frank told him. "And there isn't a fire station out here."

Joe cast an uneasy glance in the rearview mirror. "What's out on this road beside the Benders' place?"

"I don't know," Frank answered.

"Neither do I," Joe said grimly, and he pressed down on the gas pedal.

The van roared through the viaduct and around the curve on the other side. Joe barely noticed the swarm of police cruisers clustered in the driveway near the old farmhouse. The charred remains of the barn took his attention, but the flashing red light on an ambulance sent a chill down his spine.

Chapter

2

JOE SWERVED down the short stretch of road, blasted up the long driveway, slammed on the brakes, and was out the door almost before the van skidded to a halt on the loose gravel. He sprinted over to the ambulance, but a uniformed figure blocked his path. It was Officer Con Riley of the Bayport police.

"Hold it right there, Joe," Riley said in a firm, steady voice. "This is police business." He cast a brief glance at the shrouded form in the back of the ambulance. "You can't do anything for that poor guy now, anyway."

"Guy?" Joe said in a strained voice. "You're sure it's a guy?"

"Reasonably sure. The fire fighters found him in a room that wasn't burned. The smoke probably killed him. The woman who lives here identified him as a writer named Skip Guzman, and that's the name that popped up on the computer when we traced the license plates on that car over there.''

Frank put his hand on Joe's shoulder. "Vanessa's right over there," he said calmly, pointing with his other hand.

Relief washed over Joe's face, and he took off for Vanessa, leaving Frank alone with Con Riley.

"So, Con," Frank said, "what happened here?"

"What does it look like?" Riley replied. "The barn burned down with somebody inside it."

"Come on, Con," Frank prodded. "You can tell me more than that."

Riley shrugged. "Not much else to tell. We don't know the cause yet." He gestured at two bright red cars. "The fire investigators are starting to sift through the rubble now. We know the fire started sometime before one A.M. because that's when the fire department got the alarm."

"Who called it in?" Frank asked.

"Frank," Riley said with a patient smile, "leave this one to the pros, okay? If the fire was arson or if any kind of foul play was involved—"

"That would make it a murder case," Frank finished for him. "Thanks for your help, Con. I'd better go find Joe. See you later."

"That's exactly what I'm afraid of," the police officer muttered as Frank walked away.

Frank found Joe on the front porch of the house with Vanessa and her mother.

Lynn St. Pierre was there, too. All three women were staring glumly at the half of the barn that was still standing. None of them looked as if they'd gotten much sleep.

"Is there anything we can do?" Frank asked Andrea Bender.

She shook her head slowly. "No. But thanks for asking. I told him to go home. We didn't need his rewrite for a few more days." She was almost talking to herself. "It wasn't a matter of life and death—at least, it wasn't supposed to be."

"It wasn't your fault, Andrea," Lynn St. Pierre said. "It was an accident. There was nothing you could have done."

"Maybe if I had been here . . ." Andrea replied, her voice trailing off.

Vanessa spoke up in an angry voice. "Maybe if a frog had wings, it wouldn't bump its belly on the ground so much. Isn't that what you always tell me? I called the fire department as soon as I heard the smoke alarm. I ran into the studio and grabbed all the computer disks I could find."

She turned to Joe with tears in her eyes. "I didn't know Skip was in there. I couldn't see— there was so much smoke. I barely found my way back out. When I noticed Skip's car in the driveway, it was too late to go back. There were flames everywhere. What more could anyone have done?"

Before Joe could respond, Andrea Bender put her arms around her daughter. "Hey, kiddo," she said softly, "I was just feeling sorry for myself. You should be proud of what you did."

"That's right," Lynn St. Pierre said. "If 'Rex Rover' ever gets off the ground, it will be because you rescued most of the first three episodes."

Frank asked Andrea Bender, "You weren't here last night?"

"I drove into New York City to have dinner with some friends," she said. "I must have been on my way home when the fire started. By the time I got here, the fire department was already fighting the blaze."

Joe glanced over at the remains of the barn. "Is any of your equipment usable?"

"The computers and electronic gear will all be replaced by the insurance," Andrea said. "And thanks to Vanessa, we have most of the computerized animation on disk." She paused for a second. "In black and white, that is."

Joe frowned slightly. "Why not in color?"

"That was the one thing we were still doing by hand," Andrea explained. "We transfer the black-and-white art to animation cels—a kind of clear plastic film—and then colorists hand-paint them. Over half the first episode was already colored. It looked terrific."

"And I'll bet the animation cels were stored in the studio," Frank ventured.

"You'd make a good gambler," Andrea replied. "They're all smoke and ashes now."

Joe spotted a sleek silver sports car coming up the driveway. At the front of the house a heavyset man with matching silver hair got out. He stuck his hands in the deep pockets of his leather coat and trudged up the porch steps.

"I guess you got my message," Andrea said.

"That's the trouble with answering machines," the man replied. "They don't weed out the bad news."

There was an awkward silence for a moment.

"I'm Joe Hardy," Joe said, filling the gap.

"Phil Gemowski," the man replied. "You must be one of Vanessa's friends."

"I guess you could say that," Joe said with a slight smile.

The silver-haired man's gaze moved from Joe to Frank. "And you are—?"

"Frank Hardy," Frank said. "The brother of Vanessa's friend," he added. "You must be a friend of the family, too."

"I like to think so," Gemowski said, turning to Andrea.

"He's more than a friend," Andrea explained. "Phil taught me most of what I know about animation. I used to work for his company, Gem Graphics. Have you ever heard of Mega Mouse?"

"Sure!" Joe answered. "I used to watch that all the time."

"That was the first cartoon show I ever worked on," Andrea said. "Phil gave me my big break."

"I just recognized your talent and put it to use," Gemowski responded. He glanced out at the smoking wreckage. "Is it as bad as it looks?"

Andrea sighed and shrugged her shoulders. "The insurance should cover most of the physical damage. But it won't bring Skip back. It also won't cover the deadline in my contract with the television network. If I don't deliver the first episode in four weeks, they'll take the show to another animation company."

Frank was curious and asked Lynn St. Pierre, "Can the network do that without your permission? If you created 'Rex Rover,' don't you own it?"

"It's not that simple," she said. "I have a contract, too. The network controls all production decisions. I want to work with Andrea and her company, but it's not up to me."

"How could something like this happen?" Gemowski asked. "Was Skip a smoker?"

"Nobody in the studio smoked," Vanessa said. "Mom has a strict no-smoking policy."

"Then we know we can rule out at least one possible cause of the fire," Frank remarked, "unless someone was smoking without your knowing it."

Lynn St. Pierre wrapped her hands around her arms and shivered. "It's cold out here. Let's go inside."

Gemowski nodded. "Good idea."

"I'll make coffee," Andrea said. "It'll give me something to do."

"We should probably be going," Frank said to Joe. "We're already late for school."

Joe turned to Vanessa. "Are you coming?"

"I might as well," she said. "There's not much I can do around here."

They were about to get into the van when Frank heard a familiar voice. "What are you two doing here?" Police Chief Collig demanded in a loud growl.

Frank turned and put on his best smile. "Hello, Chief. Have you met Vanessa Bender? She lives here. We came by to give her a lift to school. Is there a problem?"

The police chief grunted. "There might be if you start nosing around. Practically every time there's a crime in Bayport, the two of you get involved somehow."

Frank stared at Chief Collig with keen interest. "Does that mean there's been a crime here?"

Collig scowled. "I didn't say that. We haven't found any evidence that a crime was committed. This fire was probably accidental—faulty electric wiring or something like that."

While Frank and the police chief bantered back and forth, Joe and Vanessa wandered over to a pile of charred timbers still sizzling in the wet snow. Joe nudged one of the boards with the toe of his shoe, and the flimsy heap of half-burned lumber collapsed in on itself. Joe leapt

17

back in surprise, pulling Vanessa with him. As he moved back he tripped, and they both went sprawling.

Chief Collig whirled at the commotion. "Get away from there!" he barked, glaring at Joe. "One man died here already, and that's one too many, as far as I'm concerned."

Frank helped Vanessa up and brushed the dirty snow off the back of her parka. Joe was still on the ground, not moving. At first Frank was afraid his brother might be hurt. Then he noticed that Joe was staring at something on the ground.

Joe's gloved hand reached out slowly, brushed aside some sooty embers, and closed around a small object with a dull metallic glint. He got to his feet and carefully examined his find, rubbing the surface clean. "Take a look at this," he said, holding his hand out to Frank and Vanessa. "If nobody in the studio smoked, what was *this* doing here?"

Frank scrutinized Joe's outstretched hand. Lying in the palm of his glove was a half-melted lump of shiny metal. A closer look revealed a small notched wheel like a tiny cog in a mysterious machine.

Frank and Joe shared a knowing glance, and then Frank turned to the police chief, who had joined them. "You don't see many of these any-more—but I'll bet a month's allowance that this is an old-fashioned, chrome-plated cigarette lighter."

Chapter

3

CHIEF COLLIG peered at the lumpy chunk of chrome. "You'd better give that to me," he said.

Reluctantly Joe handed him the lighter. "What are you going to do with it?"

"Give it to the fire investigators," Collig answered. "It's probably nothing, but it won't hurt to check."

Frank scanned the area around the smoldering timbers. He spotted a blackened jumble of what appeared to be paint cans. A few of them had apparently exploded in the heat of the fire, leaving nothing but jagged shards of scorched metal. "Was paint stored in the studio?" he asked Vanessa.

"Sure," Vanessa said. "You need a lot of

19

paint to color all those animation cels—and a lot of paint thinner, too.''

Frank glanced at his brother. "Are you thinking what I'm thinking?''

Joe nodded. "If I were going to torch a building, a storage room full of highly flammable paint thinner would be a great place to start.''

"Let's not jump to any conclusions, boys,'' the police chief said gruffly. "We have trained experts to handle cases like this. We also have trained experts to handle cases of truancy. Shouldn't you be in school right now?''

"That's just where we were headed when we ran into you,'' Frank replied.

Chief Collig stepped off to one side and gestured toward the Hardys' van. "Don't let me stop you.''

"I don't suppose you'd give us a note explaining why we're late,'' Joe said as he walked past the police chief.

Chief Collig smiled thinly. "You're right. I wouldn't.''

Joe was anxious to meet Vanessa after school to start working on the case. He knew Frank would want to check out the mysterious fire more closely, too. When it came to murder, the Hardys didn't believe in coincidences—and the cigarette lighter they had found near the cans of paint thinner was the kind of "coincidence" that should set off alarm bells in any detective's head.

The Hardys had a knack for solving cases that had stumped law enforcement agents. Their father, Fenton Hardy, was a private investigator and a former police officer, and they had picked up a lot just by watching him. A few times Frank and Joe cracked cases that even Fenton Hardy couldn't unravel.

Frank and Joe made a great team. Frank's logical mind uncovered a suspect's hidden motives or any holes in an airtight alibi. Joe filled in the gaps with raw nerve and instinct. Right then Joe's instincts told him the fire and the death of Skip Guzman weren't accidents.

When his last class finally ended, Joe found Vanessa waiting for him by his locker. They met Frank at the van, climbed in, and took off to look for a killer.

Their first stop was the police station. "You two stay here," Frank said. "It'll be easier if I do this alone."

Inside the station Frank knew he wouldn't get past the desk sergeant, which wasn't a problem. He didn't plan on going farther than that. "Excuse me," he said in a polite but worried tone. Frank thought the effect sounded just about right. "I got a message at school that said my brother had been in an accident. The principal told me somebody at the police station would let me in on what happened."

"What's your brother's name?" the sergeant asked, not looking up from his paperwork.

"Skip Guzman," Frank replied.

The police officer's head jerked up. "Did you say Skip Guzman?"

Frank nodded.

An uneasy look crept over the sergeant's face. "I hate to have to be the one to tell you—but your brother died in a fire last night."

Frank tried to act shocked. "A fire? Last night? What time? How did it start?"

The sergeant rummaged around on his desk and pulled out a thin file folder. "The cause of the fire is still unknown. The time of death was sometime between twelve-thirty and one-fifteen A.M."

Frank craned his head over the desk to get a glimpse of the report. "What was the cause of death?"

"Smoke inhalation," the sergeant said. "That's what kills most people in fires."

"Are you sure that's what killed him?" Frank responded.

The police officer snapped the file shut and eyed Frank warily. "Who did you say you were? You sound like a reporter to me. Let's see some ID."

Frank backed away from the desk. "I left my wallet in the car. I'll go get it."

"Hold it right there!" the sergeant shouted as Frank headed for the door.

He didn't get very far. He barely missed a head-on collision with Con Riley at the door.

"Whoa!" the police officer exclaimed. "Watch

where you're going, or I'll have to haul you in for reckless walking. And since you're already in the station, I wouldn't have to haul you very far."

"Uh, sorry, Con," Frank managed to get out.

"Do you know this guy?" the desk sergeant asked in an angry voice.

"Take it easy, Stan," Riley said in a soothing tone. "I'll handle this." He turned his gaze on Frank. "What's going on?"

Frank shrugged and smiled. "You know me, Con. Just trying to help out."

"Yeah, right," Riley said. "Since I know you won't just drop it because I ask you, I'm going to let you in on some confidential information. The forensics guys turned up something interesting on that lighter your brother found."

Frank's face lit up. "I knew it. It was arson, right?"

Riley shook his head. "The lighter was in pretty bad shape—but not bad enough to wipe out the initials *S.G.* engraved on the bottom."

Con didn't have to say any more. Frank knew what came next. "So Skip Guzman's initials were on the lighter. Does that mean the investigators think Guzman started the fire?"

"That's the best theory they have so far," Riley replied. "Maybe Guzman had a secret smoking habit. Maybe he got careless and left a lit cigarette in the wrong place when he was in the studio alone."

"Do you believe that?" Frank asked.

Riley shrugged. "I'll have to until somebody finds a better explanation."

When Frank got back to the van, he shared what he had found out with Joe and Vanessa.

"But Riley didn't say there was solid proof that Guzman accidentally started the fire," Joe observed. "Nothing I've heard so far rules out the possibility of arson."

"I don't get it," Vanessa said. "Why do you guys think somebody deliberately burned down the studio?"

"I don't know what to think yet," Frank replied. "I need facts. Let's start with motive. Who would want to burn down your mom's studio?"

"You mean who might want to kill Skip?" Vanessa responded.

"Good question," Frank said. "Maybe the fire was just a cover-up for murder. Does anybody gain anything from his death? With Skip Guzman out of the way, what happens to 'Rex Rover'?"

Vanessa shrugged. "Lynn could keep writing the show by herself."

"But she wouldn't have to split fifty-fifty with Guzman anymore," Joe pointed out. "She'd make a whole lot more money."

"Money is always a good motive," Frank remarked. "We'll have to find out if Lynn St. Pierre would really profit by Guzman's untimely exit."

Vanessa was stunned. "You're kidding, right? I *know* Lynn. She'd never do anything like that!"

"Okay, let's forget that angle for now," Joe said quickly. "What if the arsonist didn't know Guzman was in the studio? What if somebody just didn't want the show to get on the air?"

"There's a lot of competition for television ratings," Vanessa said. " 'Rex Rover' is scheduled to go up against another cartoon series, 'The Andersons,' in the same time slot on another network."

Frank frowned. "Would anyone be so worried about a new show that they'd commit arson and murder to keep it off the air? After all, nobody's even seen a single episode of 'Rex Rover' yet. It might be a complete flop."

"Gee, that's a cheerful thought," Vanessa said curtly.

Joe shot a hard look at his brother. Frank didn't realize he had just insulted Vanessa's mom. "We have to consider all the angles," he continued. "What about this Phil Gemowski guy?"

"What about him?" Vanessa countered, getting a little steamed now.

Joe reached back over the front seat and took Vanessa's hands in his. "We're just trying to help."

"I know," she said. "Sorry. I was up most of the night. This hasn't been one of my best days. But we're talking about murder and arson—most

25

guys I know talk about football and basketball. Give me a minute to catch up."

"Take your time," Joe said patiently.

"Okay," Vanessa said. "I'm all right. Now, where were we?"

"Phil Gemowski," Frank reminded her.

"My mom used to work for his animation company, Gem Graphics. A few years ago she got interested in computer animation, and Phil didn't want to go in that direction. He does some, of course—everyone has to—so my mom started her own animation studio. That was a little over a year ago," Vanessa said.

"He couldn't have been too happy about your mother's landing a big television deal," Joe said. "Every project she gets is one Gem Graphics might have had."

"You shouldn't underestimate Phil Gemowski," Vanessa responded. "He's a pretty shrewd operator. He invested a large chunk of money in my mom's company. If she makes money, so does he."

"We're not making a lot of progress," Frank commented. "So far we have exactly zero suspects. What about personal enemies? Is there anybody who has a grudge against your mom?"

Vanessa shook her head. "Not that I know of."

"Wait a minute," she said after a brief pause. "There *is* somebody who stands to lose a lot from computer animation. Most of the big animation studios farm out a lot of the repetitive detail work to companies that use cheap overseas labor.

"There's a Japanese company, Toho Enterprises, that handles a lot of those deals," she continued. "They have this really pushy sales agent in their New York office. His name is Akira Fukojima. My mom keeps telling him she doesn't need the services of his company because of her computers, but he won't take no for an answer."

Joe frowned slightly. "Do you think the guy is wacko enough to torch her studio just because your mom isn't using him?"

"No," Vanessa replied. "Maybe, if the future of his business was on the line? My mom's computer software kind of makes Toho Enterprises obsolete," she explained. "Draw a character on the screen with his right foot in front of his left; then draw another with his left foot in front of his right; hit a few keys on the keyboard, and—presto!—the character can walk all the way across the screen."

"So if your mother succeeds with her computerized animation process," Frank said, "it won't be long before other animation companies use her processes. And Fukojima would be out of a job."

"Sounds like we should check out Mr. Fukojima," Joe said, picking up the car phone. A quick call to the information operator got him the phone number in New York for Toho Enterprises. A few seconds after that he was speaking to Akira Fukojima's secretary. Joe asked a few polite questions, listened to a few polite answers, and then hung up the phone.

"Fukojima's not in the office today," he told Frank and Vanessa.

"Did you find out when he would be back?" Frank asked.

"I did better than that," Joe replied with a grin. "I found out where he is right now."

Frank glanced at his brother. "Let me guess. He's at a certain farmhouse right outside Bayport, meeting with the mother of somebody in this van."

Joe's smile faded. "You're no fun," he grumbled, and he started up the van. "It was supposed to be a surprise. If we hurry, we can catch him before he leaves."

By now Joe was familiar with the route. He checked the drivers of other cars so if Fukojima left before the Hardys reached Vanessa's house, he'd know it.

The road was deserted leading up to the viaduct, which was good because the viaduct was narrow, barely wide enough for two cars. The road curved to the right at the far end of the tunnel, and Joe tapped his horn as a friendly warning to any vehicles that might be coming around the bend and into the viaduct from the other direction.

He was still looking for cars when he drove out of the viaduct. Without warning, something large and heavy smashed into the windshield, shooting a thousand tiny cracks across the shatterproof glass.

Joe tried to keep his eyes on the road. He fought back his panic as he struggled to peer through the spreading spiderweb of cracks. It was like trying to see through frosted glass. He felt as helpless as a blind man trying to land a plane.

"Hold on!" he shouted as he gripped the steering wheel and braced himself for the crash he knew was coming even though he couldn't see it.

Chapter

4

JOE SLAMMED his foot down on the brake and pulled the steering wheel to the right. If he didn't make the curve, he wanted to take the van off the road without plowing into the path of any oncoming cars.

The tires screeched and smoked. The van skidded and bounced as it hit the bumpy shoulder. Joe kept his hands clamped on the wheel and his foot glued to the brake. He couldn't tell what was out there beyond the ruined windshield. All he could do was hold on tight and hope they didn't hit a telephone pole.

The van finally shuddered to a stop without crashing into anything. Joe managed to pry his fingers off the steering wheel, and his leg started to shake when he let up on the brake pedal. He let out a deep breath and glanced over at his brother.

"What hit us?" Vanessa asked from the back-seat, her voice barely a whisper.

"Either a jumbo jet or a giant pterodactyl would be my guess," Joe replied. His heart was still hammering, and he felt a little giddy.

"Whatever it was," Frank said, "it's probably still out there. Let's check it out."

"Fine with me," Vanessa said. "I could use some fresh air, anyway."

Frank soon found the cause of the accident. A lumpy, basketball-size slab of rock lay half buried in a snowbank on the far side of the road, about a hundred feet from the viaduct. He bent over and picked up the rock. It was heavy.

"I can see how it ended up here after hitting the van," he said as he set the rock back down on the ground. "Just imagine this is a baseball and the van is a two-ton baseball bat."

Joe closed his eyes. "Yes, I can see that. What I *can't* see is who pitched it. Somebody has to throw the ball before a batter can hit it."

Frank gazed at the railroad overpass. "No-body threw that chunk of stone. It was dropped."

Frank climbed the embankment beside the via-duct and scanned the railroad bed in both direc-tions. The fresh footprints in the snow were easy to spot. They led down the other side of the embankment to a clump of pine trees. Any four-wheel-drive vehicle could have pulled off the road and disappeared in those trees.

Even though Frank knew the culprit would be long gone, he slid down the slope to take a closer look at the shadowy stand of pines. Twin sets of wide, studded tire tracks confirmed his hunch.

Joe was carefully clearing away the last slivers of the wrecked windshield when his brother came trudging back up the road. He had smashed out the glass with a lug wrench, and used a blanket to wipe the razor-sharp glass shards out of the van.

"It'll be a bit breezy," he remarked as he inspected the job. "But at least we'll be able to see where we're going." He checked with his brother. "Did you find anything?"

"Enough to make me know that rock didn't fall off the overpass by itself," Frank replied.

"I don't get it," Joe said. "Was it some kind of prank—or is somebody out to get us?"

"Maybe somebody's out to get Vanessa, and we just happened to be in the way," Frank suggested.

Joe didn't like the sound of that. "If anybody tries to hurt Vanessa, they'll have to go through me first."

Frank took a brief look around. "Where *is* Vanessa?" he asked.

Joe jerked his thumb over his shoulder toward the farm up the road. "She walked the rest of the way home. It's only a few hundred yards."

The Hardys' battered van rolled up to the farmhouse just as a small dark-haired man in a

32

gray business suit walked out the front door. He was followed by Vanessa and her mother. The man's jaw was moving up and down at a rapid pace. It took Joe a few seconds to realize he wasn't talking—he was chewing a wad of gum.

Andrea Bender introduced the Hardys to Akira Fukojima. Fukojima smiled fiercely and kept pulverizing his gum. "Do you work for Ms. Bender?" he asked.

"No," Frank answered. "We go to school with Vanessa."

Mr. Fukojima nodded and chomped. "Ah, I see. If you'll excuse me, I must be going." He turned back to Andrea Bender. "Please think about my offer."

"If I change my mind," she said wearily, "you'll be the first to know."

Fukojima smiled some more, crushed the wad of gum between his teeth again, got in his car, and drove off.

"I thought he'd never leave," Andrea Bender murmured. She was about to go back in the house when she caught sight of the windshieldless van. "You didn't tell me you were in an accident!" she snapped at Vanessa.

"Take it easy, Mom," Vanessa said. "I'm okay. Nobody got hurt."

Andrea turned a stern gaze on Joe. "What happened?"

"Just a minor mishap with a small rock," Joe assured her.

Frank decided not to add any details to his

brother's description. Even though he was fairly sure it wasn't an accident, he didn't have a clue who had dropped the rock on the van. It might have been kids playing a prank. He didn't know if the incident was connected to the fire or what the connection might be. The only thing he knew for sure at this point was that Akira Fukojima couldn't have been standing on the top of the railroad overpass at the same time he was talking to Andrea Bender.

Nothing he could say about the "accident" would be very helpful or make Vanessa's mother feel any better. So Frank decided to change the subject. "That Mr. Fukojima certainly is—ah, interesting," he said.

Andrea rolled her eyes. "That's a polite way to put it."

"He's like some kind of vulture," Vanessa said bitterly. "The fire is barely out, and he's already hovering around, trying to pressure you into doing business his way."

"He's not that bad," her mother responded. "He's just a salesman ready for any opportunity to make a sale."

Maybe I am a fool for trying to do this on my own," she added. "I have only a handful of colorists working for me, and Fukojima has access to hundreds who'll gladly work night and day for peanuts."

"How did he find out about the studio burning down?" Joe asked.

Andrea shrugged her shoulders. "Word travels fast in the small world of animation. Akira Fukojima keeps his eyes and ears open. And if he'd just stop smacking his gum for a few seconds, he would hear me when I tell him I'm not interested in anything Toho has to offer.''

She looked at her daughter with tired eyes. "It's been a long day, kiddo, and I still have a lot of work to do. Dinner's going to be whatever I can find that won't blow up in the microwave.''

"No problem," Vanessa said. "You go ahead. I'll be in as soon as the guys leave.''

Joe cleared his throat. "Is that some kind of hint?''

Andrea Bender smiled. "Yes. My daughter is telling me to get lost so she can be alone with you.''

Vanessa's cheeks flushed. "Only because you insist on talking like that," she murmured.

After Andrea Bender went back in the house Frank decided to take the hint, too. "I'll meet you in the van," he said to Joe in a low voice.

Joe had spent most of his schoolday thinking about being alone with Vanessa. Now that it was actually happening, he couldn't think of anything to say to her.

"I appreciate all your help," Vanessa said, filling the silence that had suddenly fallen between them.

"I don't feel like I've been much help," Joe replied.

She reached out and touched his arm. "Just being a friend is a big help right now.''

Joe wanted to ask Vanessa to go out with him, but he wasn't sure if it was the right time. Part of him said to wait until things settled down; another part couldn't wait.

Frank saved him from making any kind of decision by rapping on the horn.

"Sounds like our time is up," Joe said. "I'd offer you a ride to school tomorrow, but you might freeze to death before we got there. Until we get the windshield replaced, the van's going to be a rolling refrigerator."

"That's okay," Vanessa said. "My car's supposed to be ready today. If not, my mom can give me a ride."

"We can still get together after school," Joe suggested.

Vanessa smiled warmly. "I'd like that."

Joe returned the smile. "So would I."

The major difference between the drive home and a swim in a vat of ice water, Joe reflected, was that the ice water would have felt warmer. By the time the van pulled into the driveway, Joe felt like a human Popsicle.

Their father, Fenton Hardy, was waiting for Frank and Joe when they staggered in the front door. "You two look frozen," he remarked. "What happened?"

"We'll tell you about it later," Joe said as he headed for the stairs. "Right now we both need long, hot showers."

"Not so fast," Fenton Hardy replied, shifting

to a more serious tone. "There's a man here who wants to have a talk with you."

A short, stocky man in a rumpled suit walked out of the living room and extended his right hand to Frank. "I'm Walt Steadman. So you're Fenton Hardy's boys. I've heard a lot about you. Are you Frank or Joe?"

"I'm Frank," Frank said as they shook hands.

Steadman turned to Joe. "Then you must be Joe," he said, grasping Joe's right hand and pumping it up and down. "You're the one I want to talk to."

Joe looked at his father. "Mr. Steadman is an insurance investigator," Fenton Hardy explained. "We've worked together on a few cases."

"Insurance investigator," Frank said. "Does this have anything to do with the fire at Andrea Bender's studio?"

"That's right," Steadman replied amiably. "And the sooner I clear up a few minor points, the sooner the insurance company can pay Ms. Bender's claim."

"Why do you want to talk to me?" Joe asked. "The police can tell you a lot more than I can."

"I've already talked to them," Steadman said. "Chief Collig told me about the cigarette lighter you found. I'd like to hear the story in your words."

"Do you suspect arson?" Frank asked.

The stocky man shrugged. "I get paid to be suspicious. Do *you* think the fire was arson?"

"The thought did cross my mind," Frank

said. "But what does that have to do with the insurance? Doesn't the policy pay in arson cases?"

"That depends on who the arsonist is," Steadman replied cryptically.

"You just lost me," Joe said.

"Never mind," Steadman said. "Just tell me about the lighter."

"No, wait," Frank cut in. "You already have a suspect, don't you? Who do you think started the fire?"

Steadman sighed. "I don't even know if *anybody* started the fire. The police seem to think it was an accident."

"But if it *was* arson," Joe prodded, "who do you think did it?"

Steadman studied Joe with keen, steady eyes. "I'll tell you," he said evenly. "But you may not like my answer."

"Try me," Joe said.

"Do I have to spell it out for you?" the insurance investigator responded. "You don't need to be a genius to figure out most of these insurance scams."

"I think you'd better spell it out for me," Joe said stiffly.

The insurance investigator's response was cold and blunt. "I think Andrea Bender burned down her studio to collect the insurance money."

Chapter

5

THE INSURANCE INVESTIGATOR'S words stunned Joe. Frank, on the other hand, wasn't all that surprised. Any person who walked away with the cash in a settlement was bound to be a primary suspect. Money, he reminded himself, can be a powerful motive. Still, it would take a lot to convince him.

"Explain something to me," Frank said to Steadman. "Even if Andrea Bender gets a big, fat check from the insurance company, she doesn't really make any profit on the deal. The fire destroyed her studio and most of her equipment. Even if she doesn't replace any of that stuff, all she gets is the money she paid for it in the first place."

"That's right," Joe said defiantly. "And she'd

lose her business and her career. What kind of motive does she have when you add that in?"

"You have a good point there," Steadman conceded. "But Andrea Bender had a second insurance policy—a life insurance policy on Skip Guzman for five hundred thousand dollars. How's that for a motive?"

Joe glared at the shorter man. "Are you accusing her of murder?"

"That's not my job," Steadman responded without emotion. "I just collect facts."

"Have you collected any facts that directly link Andrea Bender to the fire?" Frank challenged.

"Not yet," the insurance investigator admitted, his mouth set in a straight line. "Have *you?*"

"Now, hold on," Fenton Hardy said. "I think this conversation has gotten a little out of hand. Frank and Joe would never withhold evidence." He turned to his sons. "And Walt Steadman isn't the enemy."

"I'm sorry if I was out of line," Steadman said. "You boys don't have to tell me anything if you don't want to."

"There's nothing to tell," Joe grumbled.

"I understand," Steadman said. He handed Frank a business card. "Here's my number. Call me if you come across anything that might shed some light on this case."

"What makes you think we'll find anything you or the police don't already know?" Frank asked.

The insurance investigator chuckled. "Because I know you take after your father."

Early the next morning Frank and Joe found a note from their father on the kitchen table.

" 'I took the van to a glass company,' " Joe read aloud. " 'It should be ready this afternoon.' "

"We'll need to hitch a ride to school with someone," Frank said. "I'll call Chet Morton to see if he can give us a lift." The boys' mother and aunt Gertrude were out of town with an elderly aunt who had fallen and broken her hip.

The kitchen phone rang just as Frank was reaching for it. He answered it and then handed the receiver to his brother. "It's for you," he said.

Joe smiled when he heard Vanessa's voice. She told him she was mobile again. Her car was rolling on four brand-new tires, and she volunteered to give the Hardys a lift to school. Joe told her it was out of her way. She said she didn't mind, and he didn't give her much of an argument, because as much as he liked Chet, the big guy wasn't nearly as interesting as Vanessa Bender.

After breakfast, while they waited for Vanessa, Frank brought up a subject that had weighed on his mind all night. "You know," he began cautiously, "that life insurance policy on Skip Guzman puts a new twist in this case."

Joe raised his eyebrows. "Oh?" He knew where

41

the conversation was heading, and he didn't want to go there.

"Half a million dollars is a lot of money," Frank said.

Joe nodded. "It certainly is—and if Andrea Bender didn't have an alibi, she'd have to answer a lot of hard questions."

"We don't know if she has an alibi," Frank pointed out. "She claims she was halfway between New York City and Bayport when the fire started, but all we have is her word for it, unless she can prove what time she left the city."

"Well, maybe we should find evidence to back up her story instead of joining the lynch mob," Joe snapped hotly.

"I don't like this any more than you do," Frank said. "But we can't ignore the facts. Five hundred grand buys a lot of motive. Even if her alibi checks out, she could have hired somebody to torch the studio."

"The facts!" Joe spit out the words. "Here's a fact you haven't fed into that computer in your skull. Vanessa was almost killed in the fire along with Skip Guzman. I've seen Vanessa and her mother together, and I can tell how much they care about each other. I can't believe that Andrea Bender would knowingly put her daughter into danger."

"Andrea had no way of knowing that Vanessa would go into the burning studio," Frank argued.

"She also had no way of knowing that the

42

blaze wouldn't spread to the house!" Joe countered. "Whoever started that fire didn't care very much about Vanessa's safety. Does that sound like Andrea Bender to you?"

Frank was silent for a moment. "No, it doesn't," he finally admitted. "But I still think we should find out why she took out that huge life insurance policy on Guzman."

A car horn outside ended the discussion. "That's Vanessa," Joe said. "Let's go." He grabbed his jacket out of the front hall closet and threw Frank's coat at him. "Do me a favor," he added as they made their way out the door. "Don't mention any of this to Vanessa."

Frank glanced at his brother. "Give me a little credit, will you? I know what she's been through the last couple of days. I wouldn't add to that by telling her that her mother might be a murder suspect—even if you didn't like her so much."

"What do you mean by that?" Joe protested. "I barely know her. We're just friends."

Frank grinned. "Give it a few more days, and then try to tell me that with a straight face."

"I have to make a short detour on the way to school," Vanessa told them as Frank climbed into the back and Joe took the seat next to her in the front. "At least, I *think* it's short. I'm not completely familiar with the layout of Bayport yet." She handed Joe a sheet of paper. "My mom wrote down these directions."

Joe studied the paper for a few seconds.

43

" 'Congratulations,' " he read. " 'You have already won one of the following fabulous prizes: a brand-new sports car, a state-of-the-art home entertainment system, or a special mystery prize. . . .' "

"Try the other side," Vanessa said. "We try to get *some* use out of our junk mail."

Joe turned the paper over and scanned the handwriting. "These directions make perfect sense—if we want to drive back to your house and start from there."

"Sorry about that," Vanessa said. "Mom didn't know I was going to pick you up first. Can you figure out how to get there from here?"

Joe ignored the detailed list of streets and turns and skipped to the address scrawled at the bottom. "Ten twenty-eight Kendall Avenue. I know where that is. Hang a left at the next stop sign."

"Now that we know *where* we're going," Frank remarked, "what's there, and why are we going?"

"I have to drop off some papers at Lynn St. Pierre's house," Vanessa said.

"What kind of papers?" Frank wanted to know, eyeing a large manila envelope on the seat next to him.

"Character sketches," Vanessa replied. "Each time a new character is introduced in a script, the production artists make some preliminary drawings. Then Lynn and my mom look at the designs and decide which ones to use."

Frank picked up the envelope. "Are the sketches in here?"

"Can we look at them?" Joe added before Vanessa could answer.

"Sure," she said. "Unless you're planning to steal the designs for your own animated show."

Frank opened the envelope and pulled out a thin stack of photocopies. "These look like cartoon mug shots," he observed. Each page had several drawings of the same character, full figure and profile. Neat block letters in the margins provided height, hair color, and other information. He leafed through the pile and picked out one that caught his eye. The bushy eyebrows, fat nose, and large, protruding ears were exaggerated to make the character more comical, but Frank could tell who was lurking under the caricature. "Take a look at this one," he said, handing the drawing to Joe.

"Hey!" Joe exclaimed in delight. "This is Police Chief Collig!"

"Mom did that one herself," Vanessa said.

"I didn't know she was an artist," Joe replied.

"That's how she got into this business," Vanessa explained. "She started out doing character designs and conceptual drawings for Gem Graphics. She's come a long way since then."

"I'd like to hear more about it," Frank said.

"It'll have to wait," Joe said abruptly. "I think the next house on the right is ours."

Vanessa pulled over to the curb and parked. Frank and Joe got out of the car with her.

"Gee, thanks, guys," she said with a playful smile as they walked her up to the small frame house, "but I think I can do this without an escort."

"I just needed to get out and stretch," Frank said. "That backseat of yours is a little cramped."

Vanessa glanced at Joe. "Do you go anywhere without him?"

Joe shot a dirty look at his brother. "Not recently," he muttered.

Vanessa rang the doorbell, and they waited. She rang again, and they waited some more. She tried knocking and accidentally pushed the door open a few inches. "That's weird," she said. Her nose wrinkled, and a grimace creased her face. "Yuck! What's that smell?"

Frank sniffed the air. "Gas!" he exclaimed, reaching over Vanessa's shoulder to push the door open all the way. He dashed inside.

Joe yanked Vanessa out into the yard. "Go next door and call the fire department and an ambulance!" he shouted, sprinting back to the house.

The air inside made Joe gag. It was thick with the foul odor of gas. He staggered into the living room and spotted Frank in a short hallway, dragging a limp Lynn St. Pierre out of another room.

"Open some windows!" Frank croaked.

Joe flung open a window—only to discover that there was a storm window beyond it, bolted on from the outside. He grabbed a floor lamp and smashed out the glass. Gulping in some fresh air, he ran over to help his brother.

"Let's get out of here!" he yelled.

Frank could only nod. The poisoned air was starting to make him woozy. He knew he was only a few seconds from passing out. He also knew the deadly gas could kill in more than one way. If the gas reached the furnace in the basement, the flames from the furnace would ignite the gas, and they'd all be vaporized in an explosive fireball.

Together Frank and Joe carried the unconscious woman out of the house. Frank stumbled and collapsed in the snow. "We need to get farther away from the house!" he gasped, struggling to get up.

Too late Joe realized the meaning of Frank's desperate words. There was a deafening blast. Something slammed into him, lifted him off the ground, and spun him around. He came down hard, a sharp white pain burst in his skull, and the world went black.

Chapter

6

FRANK THREW HIMSELF on top of Lynn St. Pierre to shield her body with his. He covered his head with his hands as a shower of debris rained down. He lay motionless for a few seconds after the blast and then jumped up to search frantically for his brother.

When he saw Joe sprawled facedown on the ground a dozen feet away, Frank ran over and gently rolled him over. There was an ugly purple bruise on Joe's forehead. Frank couldn't see any other injuries.

Joe moaned softly, and his eyes fluttered open. "Somebody get the license number of that truck," he groaned.

"That was no truck," Frank said. "It was the shock wave from the explosion." He glanced back at the house. It could have been worse, he thought. Most of the house was still standing—but not for long. One side was completely gone, and another wall canted outward at an awkward angle. If the structure didn't collapse on its own, a wrecking crew would have to finish the job. A few pockets of flame burned fitfully. The force of the blast had snuffed out most of the fire the instant it had begun.

Joe struggled to a sitting position and, with Frank's help, stood up groggily. He took a few experimental steps and groaned. It was a strange sensation, almost as if the groan had come from outside his body. Another groan drifted by, and this time Joe was sure it hadn't come from him.

Frank and Joe whirled around to focus on Lynn St. Pierre. She was on her hands and knees, trying to stand. The Hardys rushed over to help her up.

"Are you okay?" Frank asked.

"What happened?" she rasped, her voice a choked whisper.

"There was a gas leak," Frank explained.

"A big one," Joe added.

Lynn stared blankly at the remains of her house. "I guess so," she responded, obviously not taking in the full situation.

Vanessa came running across the lawn from the house next door with a heavy coat and boots. "Are you all right?" she asked all of them, slipping Lynn's feet into the boots and laying the coat over her shoulders.

Joe touched his throbbing forehead. "I've been better—but at least we're all alive."

"That's a minor miracle," Vanessa replied, eyeing the gaping hole where the front door had been.

"I think we should all go next door to get warm until the fire fighters and police come," Frank said. No one moved to leave Lynn's front yard.

"Is this what happens when the pilot light on the stove goes out?" Vanessa asked.

"No," Frank said. "A pilot doesn't use much gas. There was enough gas in there to—well, blow up a house."

"And there weren't any pilot lights to go out," Lynn said. "The gas furnace had an electronic ignition. The stove was practically an antique. I had to light it by hand."

"If you turned on the oven," Joe ventured, "and forgot to light it, that would flood the house with enough gas to blow the roof off."

"Good theory," Lynn replied. "The only trouble is, I don't cook. I was just renting this house and only had one saucepan."

"And even if you accidentally turned on the gas," Vanessa said, "you'd have noticed the smell."

"Not if she was asleep," Frank noted.

"To the best of my knowledge," Lynn said, "I'm not a suicidal, sleepwalking chef."

"Too bad," Joe remarked. "That would clear up a lot of questions."

"That's not what I meant," Frank said seriously. "The front door was unlocked. Anybody could have gone in during the night and turned on the gas."

"Who'd want to?" Lynn asked.

"Whoever wants to stop the production of 'Rex Rover,' " Frank answered.

"With both writers dead," Joe pointed out, "the show would be dead, too."

"Not necessarily," Lynn said. "Skip and I created the show, but that doesn't mean nobody else could write it—and Andrea wouldn't even have to worry for a while."

"What do you mean?" Frank asked.

"Skip and I already finished the scripts for the first six episodes," Lynn told him.

A siren wailed nearby. "What took them so long?" Joe grumbled.

The street was soon crawling with fire engines and police cars. Chief Collig had a brief conversation with Lynn St. Pierre before an ambulance whisked her off to the hospital for a checkup, despite her protests. Then the police chief turned his attention to the Hardys.

"There's not going to be much left of this town when you two get through with it," he said sourly. "Why is it that I always run into you at the scene of major disasters?"

"Coincidence?" Joe suggested.

Chief Collig scowled. "Somehow I doubt that. What were you doing here?"

"They were with me," Vanessa answered.

51

She explained the whole situation to the police chief. Her explanation didn't seem to make him any happier.

"You boys could have been killed in there," Chief Collig said gravely.

"If we'd stayed out here," Frank replied, "Lynn St. Pierre definitely would have been killed in there."

The police chief let out a sigh to vent some of his frustration. "That's not the point. I know you boys mean well, but I can't condone your junior detective antics. One of these days you're going to get seriously hurt." He stopped and took a closer look at Joe. "What happened to your head?"

Joe put his hand up to cover the dark bruise on his forehead.

"A completely unrelated incident," Frank asserted. "He's been training for luge. Nobody told him you need a special kind of sled—and a crash helmet."

"Or that you're supposed to go down the hill feet first," Vanessa chipped in, grinning mischievously.

The police chief threw his hands up in disgust. "I give up! I'm going to get an officer to take your statements. After that I want you out of my sight. Are we clear on that?"

"Crystal clear," Joe assured him.

"Just one question," Frank said.

Chief Collig glared at him. "What?"

"Do you still think the fire at Andrea Bender's studio was an accident?"

The police chief put his hands on his hips. "I'm not getting through to you, am I? I know what you're thinking, and you can forget it. The investigation didn't turn up anything definite. The lighter with the initials *S.G.* is the only solid clue we have—and even if we could link it to the fire, which we can't, it still reads like an accident.

"And furthermore," he continued forcefully, "even if the fire wasn't an accident and there's some connection between the fire and this explosion, the police department will handle it—*not* the police and their pals Frank and Joe Hardy. Got it?"

"Does that mean we're not pals anymore?" Joe asked innocently.

Chief Collig's eyes flicked between the two brothers. "Great," he said. "Why can't you guys do what other kids do? Don't you play football or baseball or anything like that?"

"It's the middle of winter," Joe said. "Hockey or basketball would be more like it."

"Don't forget the luge," Vanessa reminded him.

Joe rubbed his throbbing head. "How could I?"

The police chief started to say something, then changed his mind, spun around, and stomped off.

"I don't think he was happy to see us," Joe observed.

* * *

53

After school Joe found a note from Frank in his locker. Frank liked to break into Joe's locker and leave him little notes. Most of them were along the lines of "Gotcha!" Joe kept changing his lock, but Frank successfully kept picking it. Usually he timed himself. So sometimes the notes would say something like "Only twenty-three seconds!" That day's note was a little more informative.

"I left early to pick up the van," the note told him. "If I'm not back when you get out of class, wait for me." There was a scribble at the bottom that might have been Frank's signature. It also might have been "Fringe" or "Flake" or any other word that started with the letter *F*. Penmanship was not one of Frank's strong points.

Joe didn't have to wait. The black van was parked in front of the school when he strolled out.

"So where are we going?" he asked as he climbed into the passenger seat.

"No place in particular," Frank said, shifting the van into gear and rolling down the street. "Not yet, anyway. We need to talk."

Joe studied his brother. Frank studied the road.

"Okay," Joe said. "Let's talk."

"We don't have a lot of suspects," Frank began, "but two of them are close to Vanessa."

"Well, I don't think Lynn St. Pierre is much of a suspect anymore," Joe responded. "Unless you think she decided to cover her tracks by blowing herself up."

"I've been giving that some thought," Frank said. "She could have faked the whole thing to throw suspicion off herself. After all, if we think somebody's trying to kill her, then we would probably assume it's the same person who killed Skip Guzman."

"Which we did," Joe pointed out.

"That just proves my point," Frank replied.

"Wait a minute," Joe said. "Don't you think killing yourself is sort of a drastic way to avoid suspicion of murder?"

"Maybe something went wrong," Frank suggested. "Maybe she didn't realize how fast the gas fumes would fill the house. She might have been overcome before she could get out."

Joe cast a sidelong glance at his brother. "That's a little farfetched, don't you think?"

"Sure," Frank readily admitted. "But it's possible."

"Okay," Joe said. "But what about the rock that somebody heaved at the van? How does that fit in?"

"It doesn't," Frank conceded. "Not yet, anyway."

"So where do we go from here?" Joe asked.

Frank paused and chose his words carefully. "We really need to talk to Andrea Bender about that insurance policy—and while we're at it, we should try to find out if she took out a similar life insurance policy on Lynn."

Joe sighed. "I guess you're right—but we should check out Phil Gemowski, too. Don't forget, he owns a chunk of Andrea's company. In fact, I think we should question him before we bother Andrea."

"I think your judgment might be a little clouded by the way you feel about Vanessa," Frank said bluntly.

"I don't know what I feel about her!" Joe shot back.

Frank pulled the van over to the side of the road, stopped, and turned to his brother. "Let's start over. I'm not out to hang Andrea Bender. I hope she can tell us something that will definitely clear her and lead us to Guzman's killer. Okay?"

Joe was silent for a long time. "Okay," he finally said. "Let's get it over with."

Frank checked the side mirrors and the rear-view mirror before pulling back out onto the road. Other than a brown sedan parked on the shoulder about fifty yards behind them, the road was clear. When the van started moving, so did the sedan. A warning light flashed in Frank's head, and he made an abrupt right turn at the next corner.

"What's going on?" Joe asked. "This isn't the way to the Benders' house."

"I know," Frank said grimly, glancing in the mirror. The brown sedan rounded the corner behind them. "We've being followed."

Chapter
7

FRANK STEPPED on the gas, and the brown sedan dwindled in size in the rearview mirror. He made a quick left turn, the van's tires screaming in protest. The road led away from town, toward the cliffs by Barmet Bay. There were only a few houses out that way, and almost no traffic.

Frank's eyes darted to the mirror. There was no sign of the brown car. He eased up on the gas.

"Did we shake him?" Joe asked.

"I don't know," Frank answered. "I don't see him back there."

"Then he probably can't see us, either," Joe said. "Make another turn before he has a chance to spot us."

"Good idea," Frank said. He scanned the road ahead on both sides. "Except there's no place to turn off." His eyes moved to the mirror, and his foot nudged the gas pedal.

Joe glanced over at his brother. "Do we have company again?"

Frank nodded.

Joe crawled into the back of the van to peer out the rear window. "An old brown sedan that looks like it hasn't been washed for a few years?"

"That's it," Frank said.

Joe kept his eye on the car. It was too far away for him to read the license plate. "Slow down," he said. "Let him catch up."

Frank let the speedometer needle fall back. "Why do you want to do that?" he asked.

Joe watched the car behind them gain a little and then back off again. "That person knows how to follow," he said. "Do you think you can lose him?"

Frank spotted a gas station up ahead. 'I've got a better idea," he replied. He pulled into the station and drove up to one of the pumps.

"Great time to run out of gas," Joe grumbled.

Frank glanced at the fuel gauge. The tank was almost full. "We don't need gas," he said.

Joe turned his head to his brother. "Then what are we doing here?"

"Waiting," Frank replied.

Joe looked back out the rear window. The

brown sedan cruised by without even slowing down.

Frank watched the action in the side-view mirror. "He doesn't want us to know he's following us," he said. "So he can't be too obvious."

Joe climbed back into the front seat. "So what do we do now? We can't stay here all day."

"Don't worry," Frank said as he steered the van back onto the road. "I've got a plan."

"I hate it when you say that," Joe muttered.

Frank smiled. "Trust me."

"That's what you always say—right after you say 'Don't worry, I've got a plan.' Then you make me do something stupid like impersonate a sewer inspector."

Frank ignored his protests and pointed up the road. "I guarantee this plan will work. Check it out."

Joe saw that they were closing in on the brown sedan. "I get it," he said with a grin. "Now we tail *him*."

"Something like that," Frank said vaguely.

A traffic light ahead shifted from green to yellow. Suddenly Frank stomped on the gas pedal, swerved into the left lane, and darted past the sedan. Then he cut back into the right lane and hit the brakes just as the red light blinked on. The car behind them screeched to a halt inches from the van's rear bumper.

Joe stared at his brother. "This is your great plan?"

"That was phase one," Frank explained. "You get to handle phase two."

"What's that?" Joe responded, almost shouting. "Go out there with the lug wrench and remove a couple of his tires so he can't follow us anymore?"

"You got the first part right," Frank said calmly. "But you won't need the lug wrench. Just get out and take a close look at the driver."

"Terrific," Joe grumbled, shoving the door open. He trudged around to the back of the van and put on a halfhearted act of checking one of the rear tires while he studied the dirty brown sedan out of the corner of his eye.

The low late-afternoon sun created a white glare on the windshield, making it hard to see inside. Joe moved to the other side of the van and pretended to check that tire, too, hoping to get a better glimpse of the driver from a different angle. The driver made the job easy for him by getting out.

"I should have known it was you," Joe said to the short man in the rumpled trenchcoat. "Is this how all insurance investigators work—following other people around, hoping they'll do all their work for them?"

"I don't know," Walt Steadman replied. "I don't pay much attention to what other investigators do. Is this how all teenagers drive—speeding up for yellow lights and not going on green?"

Joe glanced over his shoulder. The traffic light was green, and the van wasn't moving.

"Why don't we pull over to the side of the road and have a little chat?" Steadman suggested.

Frank grabbed two ski caps from the back of the van and put his gloves on before he got out of the van to face Steadman. He tossed one of the caps to Joe and put on the other one himself. With the hat, gloves, and his ski parka, Frank barely felt the chill winter air.

"So why were you following us?" he bluntly asked the insurance investigator.

"Interesting things seem to happen around you," Steadman answered.

"You heard about what happened at Lynn St. Pierre's house," Joe said.

Steadman nodded. "I wanted to talk to you about that. I drove over to the school to catch you when you got out."

"But you changed your mind and decided to tail us instead," Frank said.

Steadman shrugged. "I figured it was worth a shot."

"I take it you haven't turned up much on your own," Joe said.

"I checked out Andrea Bender's alibi," Steadman revealed. "Based on the time her friends claim she left the city, she could have gotten back in time to start the fire. She would have had to stretch a few speed limits to do it, but it's possible."

Steadman paused and shivered. "What about you guys?" he asked, hunching his shoulders and thrusting his hands deeper into the pockets of his thin trenchcoat. "Have you come up with anything?"

"You look like you're freezing," Frank said in a concerned tone. "Maybe you should get back in your car and warm up."

The insurance investigator snorted. "And then you guys take off without telling me anything."

Frank smiled. "You catch on pretty quickly. And don't bother trying to tail us again. If you do, we'll just drive around in circles all afternoon."

"Or we could go to a movie," Joe said cheerfully. *"Ninja Warlords from Neptune* is playing over in Lewiston."

"Okay," Steadman muttered, his teeth clattering. "You win. I've had enough for one day."

When the Hardys got to the Benders' house, Andrea was outside directing a couple of burly delivery men unloading large boxes from a truck.

"What's all this?" Frank asked. "New furniture?"

Andrea chuckled. "There's no room for furniture. In fact, I cleared everything out of the first floor that wasn't nailed down." She patted one of the boxes. "These are the salvation of 'Rex Rover.' "

Joe took a close look at one of the boxes. "Fragile!" a sticker warned. "Sensitive electronic components!"

"New computers?" he ventured.

"Well, I don't know how new they are," Andrea said. "It's all rental equipment—but as long as they hold up until the insurance check comes in and I can buy new stuff, things may work out okay.''

Frank cleared his throat. "Speaking of insurance, a guy who works for the insurance company paid us a visit.''

Andrea raised her eyebrows. "Oh? What did he want?''

"I'm not sure,'' Frank hedged. "He wanted to talk to us about the lighter Joe found—and he mentioned something about a life insurance policy on Skip Guzman.''

Andrea stared at him blankly for a moment. Then the color drained out of her face and she sat down heavily on the porch steps. "Oh, no— you mean they think— Oh, this is terrible.''

"I'm sure it's nothing,'' Joe said quickly. "Just routine. You know how insurance companies are.''

"Now that you've been dragged into this,'' Andrea said, "I think you deserve an explanation. When I got the contract to produce 'Rex Rover' my business was a small operation. I didn't have nearly enough equipment or space or people to do the job.

"Buying this place,'' she continued, "converting the barn, and getting all the equipment— all that took a lot of money.''

"More than you had,'' Frank said.

Andrea nodded. "I convinced Phil Gemowski to invest in the company, but that wasn't enough. I had to take out a bank loan for the rest. Since I was betting everything on this project, the bank insisted on the insurance coverage. It's something called key man insurance."

"Does that mean there's a life insurance policy on Lynn St. Pierre, too?" Frank asked.

"Yes," Andrea said. "And there's one for me, too."

Joe frowned. "How can you collect on the policy if you're dead?"

Andrea smiled faintly. "My company collects. If I die and the company folds, the bank liquidates the assets—which means the bank picks up the insurance check."

"This sounds like a cheery subject," a new voice remarked.

Joe spun around and found himself staring into Vanessa's deep gray-blue eyes.

"Did you come out here to sell my mom insurance or to see me?" she asked coyly.

"Actually, I came out here to sell you insurance," Joe replied. "Do you want to hear my pitch?"

"Only if you want to pitch while we walk," she said. "I'm going to take a hike in the woods."

"Sounds like fun," Frank said. "I'll join you."

Joe sighed. "That figures. Oh, well, let's go."

"See you later, Mom," Vanessa called.

The woods started about thirty yards behind the old farmhouse. Frank noted that the snowy field between the house and the tree line was crisscrossed with tracks.

"Does anybody else go back into the woods?" he asked.

Vanessa laughed. "Most of the people who work for my mom are transplanted city folk. They think man-eating bears are lurking behind every tree. Most of these tracks belong to me or my mom or the police officers who were walking around after the fire."

"You know," Frank said as they entered the shelter of the trees, "if I were going to sneak up on the farm to set the barn on fire, I'd come through these woods."

"The police must have had the same idea," Joe observed. "There are footprints all over the place."

"I think hunters illegally track deer back here," Vanessa said. "Sometimes we hear gunshots."

Frank stopped and scanned the area. "The trick is to find the right spot—one where you can watch the house without being seen."

He wandered into a thick stand of pine trees, where the snow had been trampled. The setting sun barely pierced the cover of green branches.

"I can't even see you from here!" Joe called out. "It's a fairly safe bet nobody could see you from the house."

"No good!" Frank shouted back. "I can't see the house!"

"Maybe not from the ground," Vanessa responded. "But who says our caller had to be on the ground?"

"Nobody," Frank said to himself. He peered

THE HARDY BOYS CASEFILES

up into the branches, picked out a tall tree with footprints around its base, and started climbing. A few minutes later he was nestled in a high branch with a perfect view of the house and the barn.

"There's something down here you should see!" Joe yelled up at him.

Frank worked his way back down the tree and joined Joe and Vanessa on the ground. "Did you find something?" he asked.

"This fluttered down while you were climbing up," Joe said, handing his brother a thin strip of colored paper. "It was probably lying on a branch and was shaken loose."

Frank looked at the piece of paper. It was a chewing gum wrapper.

"If I were looking for gum-chewing suspects," Joe said, "I'd start with Akira Fukojima."

Chapter

8

"WE'LL NEED more than a gum wrapper to make a case against Fukojima," Frank said. "We don't even know what brand of gum he chews." He took a clear plastic bag out of his coat pocket and dropped the gum wrapper inside.

Vanessa looked at Joe. "Your brother is weird," she whispered. "Does he always carry around evidence bags?"

"I heard that," Frank said. "It's just a sandwich bag. My lunch was in it."

"We're heavily into recycling at home," Joe told Vanessa.

Frank crouched down and examined the prints around the tree. "These tracks look as if they were made by hiking boots. Our footprints are pretty smooth because our shoes don't have heavy tread patterns. But these tracks have deep grooves running through them."

Joe noted how the tracks vanished into the trees. "I see what you mean. Let's follow them and see where they go."

Vanessa looked up into the sky. "We'd better hurry. We're losing the light. The sun's going down."

The tracks continued farther back into the woods. Frank led the way, scanning the ground for any other evidence that might have been left behind. They lost the trail once when the tracks crossed more footprints. After a minute of frantic searching, they picked up the distinctive tread pattern again.

The trail led to an unplowed access road that wasn't much more than a wide path.

"It looks like somebody came through here on a snowmobile," Joe said, eyeing the thick parallel tread lines that were ground deeply into the churned-up snow.

"Somehow I just can't see Akira Fukojima on a snowmobile," Vanessa remarked.

"You don't have to," Frank said. He followed the trail of footprints to the other side of the narrow road. "These tracks over here were made by a car." He stooped down to study the ground. "The footprints stop here. See? There's a little jumble of overlapping prints, just like you'd expect from somebody getting into and out of a car." He stood up and went through the motions of opening and closing a car door.

"That car had some fairly hefty snow tires," Joe observed.

Frank nodded. "It's an interesting tread pattern." He turned to Vanessa. "Do you have a water spray bottle and some aluminum foil?"

Vanessa gave him a strange look. "Not on me."

"I think he meant back at the house," Joe said.

"I'm pretty sure we do," Vanessa said. "It might take a while to find them, though. Since my mom started turning the house into a makeshift studio, I don't know where anything is."

"I'll help you," Joe offered.

"I'll stay here," Frank said.

"He's definitely weird," Vanessa whispered to Joe as they started back toward the house.

"I heard that," Frank called out after them.

After Joe and Vanessa returned with Frank's stuff, they watched with the help of flashlights as Frank pumped a fine spray of mist over the tire tread marks. He waited a minute or so, lightly touched the snow with his finger, and then sprayed the area again. He did it three or four times, until he seemed satisfied with the result.

"That should be firm enough," he said as he unrolled a sheet of aluminum foil.

"Firm enough for what?" Vanessa asked.

"I'm making a mold of the tire tread," Frank

explained as he spread out the foil on the glazed snow.

"He had to harden the tracks with a thin layer of ice before he could make the impression," Joe explained. "Otherwise he'd have mashed the snow out of shape." He sounded as if he knew what he was talking about. Actually, he had just figured it out himself—but he wasn't going to tell Vanessa that.

Slowly and delicately Frank molded the foil into the tire track, using the tips of his fingers to trace the tread grooves, making a maze of creases in the foil. "That's the best I can do," he finally said as he peeled the foil off the snow.

Joe shone his flashlight directly on his brother's handiwork. "You're a true artist," he said with a smile. "Now what do we do with it?"

"Handle it very carefully, for starters," Frank replied. "We should put it in a box or something."

"And then what?" Vanessa asked. "Take it to the police?"

Frank shook his head. "No, not yet. We need something more substantial. We need to prove that Fukojima's car made these tracks."

"We need his car to do that," Joe said.

"That won't be a problem," Vanessa informed them. "I heard my mom talking to him on the phone this afternoon. He's going to stop by the house tomorrow."

The next day was much warmer than it had been in weeks. Frank was grateful for the break from the cold—and for the thick fog that the new weather front brought with it. The van was almost invisible in the gray mist, twenty yards from the Benders' driveway.

Joe glanced at the dashboard. The numbers 3:23 glowed softly on the face of the digital clock. "If Vanessa was right about the time," he said restlessly, "Fukojima should have been here by now."

"He probably got stuck in traffic," Frank replied. "This fog is slowing everything down." He peered out the windshield. He could barely make out the dim outline of the Benders' mailbox on the side of the road. If he hadn't known it was there, he wouldn't have spotted it.

Just then two fuzzy dots of light floated in the fog beyond the mailbox. "This could be him now," Frank said.

The fuzzy dots soon turned into headlights that abruptly swerved off the road. Frank heard the muffled crunch of tires as they rolled onto gravel, and he caught a glimpse of faint red taillights as the car slowly made its way up the long, unpaved driveway.

"Let's go," Joe said eagerly, reaching for the door handle.

Frank grabbed his brother's arm. "Not so fast. Give him a few minutes to get inside the house."

A few minutes ticked by on the clock.

"Okay," Frank finally said, reaching behind

71

the seat for a cardboard box lying on the floor of the van. "Let's do it."

They padded quietly along the side of the road and then up the driveway, Joe in the lead, Frank hugging the box to his chest.

Joe squinted into the soupy mist. The hazy silhouette of the farmhouse came into view— along with a cluster of other vague shapes. Joe stopped short in his tracks, and Frank almost crashed into him.

"What's going on?" Frank hissed.

"We forgot one minor point," Joe whispered, gesturing toward the house. "Andrea is running her business out of the house, and her employees drive to work."

Now Frank could see what his brother was talking about. "There must be at least seven other cars parked there," he said in a low voice.

"I count nine," Joe responded. "I don't suppose you remember what Fukojima's car looks like."

Frank shook his head. Then he got an idea. "I know how to find the one we're looking for."

He crept up to the nearest car and put his hand on the hood. The metal was cold. He did the same thing with the next two cars and got the same result. But the fourth one was different. "This is Fukojima's car," he said confidently. "The engine's still warm."

Frank set the box on the ground and took out the strip of molded aluminum foil. It took only a few seconds to compare the mold to the tires on the car. "Not even close," he told his brother. "These tread patterns are completely different."

"He could have changed the tires," Joe suggested. "Or maybe he used another car."

"Either way," Frank replied, "we still don't have any hard evidence."

"What's going on here?" a shrill voice interjected. Frank and Joe whirled around and faced a small, agitated man.

"Oh, hi, Mr. Fukojima," Frank said, trying to sound casual. "Your left front tire's a little low. You should put some air in it."

The salesman stormed down the porch steps and jabbed his finger at the aluminum foil in Frank's hands. "What is this?" he demanded, his voice rising to a shout.

"Evidence in a murder investigation," Joe snapped, shoving the saleman's hand away from the fragile tire mold.

"Murder?" Fukojima sputtered. "What are you talking about?"

"You know what I'm talking about!" Joe shot back.

"I don't." Another voice spoke up. "Maybe you can explain it to me." Andrea Bender stood in the doorway of the old farmhouse, a mixture of confusion and anger in her face. Vanessa stood behind her, peering around her mother and giving Joe an apologetic look.

"This is a great insult," Fukojima said stiffly. "Do you suspect me in the death of Mr. Guzman? If so, you should know that I was in Los Angeles when the unfortunate event occurred." He turned to Andrea. "I am a simple business-man. One of your competitors wants very much to make an exclusive arrangement with me. I think now that I should accept his offer."

He took out a fresh stick of gum and popped it in his mouth. Frank glanced at the wrapper. It didn't match the one that Frank had stashed in his plastic bag.

"Have a nice day, and drive carefully!" Joe called out as Fukojima drove off into the fog.

"I'm sorry if we caused any trouble," Frank said to Andrea.

Before she could respond there was a sharp horn blast, and a delivery truck rumbled up to the house.

The driver hopped out of the cab, a clipboard in one hand. "That was a close one," he said. "I almost smacked head-on into some guy blast-ing out of your driveway." He studied his clip-board for a moment. "Which one of you is Andrea Bender?"

Andrea raised her hand. "That would be me."

"What is it?" Vanessa asked.

The man strolled around to the back of the truck, swung open the cargo doors, and climbed inside. "Give me a hand here, will ya?" he called out. "This thing's heavy."

"More computer equipment?" Joe guessed as he and the driver wrestled a large crate out of the truck and onto the ground.

The delivery man chuckled. "Better be careful with this piece of equipment—it has big teeth."

Frank noticed a row of air holes near the top of the crate. "I don't think that's a computer, Joe."

The crate responded with an enthusiastic bark.

Joe jumped back in surprise. "There's a dog in there!"

"This is some kind of mistake," Andrea said. "I didn't order a dog."

The delivery man handed her a slip of paper.

"Well, I'll be—" Andrea murmured as she read. "It's from the television network. They thought I could use the dog for motion studies."

"What's a motion study?" Joe asked.

"We look at a lot of film and video clips of animals in motion," Andrea explained. "It helps us make the animated movements look natural. And since Rex Rover is a dog—"

She was interrupted by the sound of the truck engine roaring to life. "Hey! Wait a minute!" she shouted.

The delivery man just smiled and waved out the window as he pulled away from the house and was swallowed by the mist.

Frank unlatched the crate lid, lifted it off, and stumbled backward as a large, friendly German shepherd bounded out and licked his face.

"I think he likes you," Joe said. "I wonder what his name is."

Frank studied the dog's collar. "He's got some kind of tag. Maybe his name's on it."

The German shepherd sat obediently as Frank parted its fur and grasped a flat metal disk attached to its collar. A faint, high-pitched whine sounded in Frank's ear. "What's that noise?" he said.

"I don't hear anything," Joe replied.

Frank suddenly became aware of another, more disturbing noise. The dog let out a low, mean growl, and its lips curled back in a vicious snarl—just before it lunged for Frank's throat.

Chapter

9

FRANK LURCHED BACK, slipped on a patch of ice, and crashed down hard on his side. An angry mass of fur and teeth bolted over him, jaws snapping shut in the air where Frank had been standing a second earlier.

The dog spun around on the driveway and charged him again. Frank scraped up a handful of gravel and flung it at the animal. The dog flinched and snarled. Frank leapt to his feet and smashed a solid side kick into the dog's jaw. The animal shook off the blow, bared its teeth, and growled.

"This dog's gone crazy!" Vanessa shouted from the side of the driveway where she and her mother looked on in horror.

Frank whipped off his ski jacket and

wrapped it around his left arm. He thrust his arm at the German shepherd, and the dog went for it, clamping its jaws shut on Frank's forearm, sinking its fangs deep into the heavy padding. The crazed animal whipped its head furiously from side to side, yanking Frank off balance and almost ripping his arm out of the socket. Frank could feel the sharp tips of the dog's teeth working their way through the layers of fabric. He jerked his arm back forcefully and left the dog crouching with a mouthful of cloth.

That was the opening Joe had been waiting for. He rushed in, holding the empty crate upside down, and slammed it over the enraged beast. He hopped on top of it while the dog spent its fury smashing against the sides and barking wildly. When the racket finally subsided Frank peered in through one of the air holes. The exhausted animal had simply gone to sleep.

"I was wrong," Joe said. "That dog doesn't like you at all."

"He seemed nice enough at first," Frank reflected, "until the noise started."

"What noise?" Joe responded.

Frank looked over at Vanessa and Andrea Bender. "Did either of you hear it?"

Vanessa shook her head.

"I didn't hear anything unusual," Andrea told him.

"It was some type of high-pitched tone,"

Frank said. "I could barely hear it. If none of you heard it, I must have been closer to the source."

Vanessa bent down and picked something up off the ground. "Here. You must have pulled this off the dog without realizing it."

In her outstretched hand Frank saw the metal disk that had been attached to the dog's collar. Frank inspected it closely. The disk was about the size and thickness of two or three quarters stacked together. Frank couldn't detect any markings on the disk, but there were two tiny screws on one side. He walked over to his van, took out a tool kit, and removed a small, slender screwdriver. Carefully Frank removed the screws and pried the cover off the disk.

"Check this out," he said to his brother. Inside the disk there were a miniature circuit board, a few colored wires, a power cell battery, and a thin, round metal object with a small hole in the top.

Frank tapped the hollow piece of metal. "I took apart a musical birthday card once. It had something like this inside."

"What is it?" Joe asked.

"A tone generator," Frank answered. "But instead of playing 'Happy Birthday,' this one emits a high-frequency signal. It was wired to go off when somebody touched it. The faint electric current in my fingers triggered it—and the dog was trained to attack on that signal."

Andrea Bender stared at him in wide-eyed shock. "What are you saying?"

"Call the television network," Frank suggested. "I'll bet nobody there sent this dog or knows anything about it."

"I think I'll do that," she said in a flat, detached voice.

"I don't get it," Vanessa said when her mother went into the house. "You think somebody sent the dog to attack my mother?"

Frank nodded. "It looks that way."

"Then why did it go after you?" she asked.

"Because I was the one who touched the dog first," Frank replied.

Andrea Bender came back out a few minutes later. "You were right," she told Frank. "The network didn't send the dog."

"Then who did?" Joe wondered out loud.

Frank looked at Andrea. "Fukojima mentioned something about one of your competitors. Do you know who he was talking about?"

"I have a fairly good idea," Andrea said. " 'Rex Rover' is scheduled for the same time slot as a show called 'The Andersons.' The show's producer, Bert Zall, has a real cutthroat reputation."

"I'd like to find out more about him," Frank said.

"There was an article about him in last month's *Animation News*," Vanessa responded. "I was just reading it the other day. I'll go get it."

Andrea smiled as her daughter bounded up the

porch steps. "She knows more about what's going on in the cartoon business than I do."

Frank and Joe took the magazine home with them. Joe scanned the article while Frank drove.

"Zall used to have two partners," Joe informed his brother. "He managed to get rid of both of them and take over Tadd, Zall, Falk Productions. He also forced a couple of smaller animation companies out of business by hiring away their best talent and forcing free-lance artists and colorists to sign exclusive contracts."

"He sounds like a real lovable guy," Frank remarked dryly.

"He looks like a sweetheart, too."

"There's a picture?"

When Frank stopped at a red light, Joe handed him the magazine. On the open page there was a small color photograph of a man with hard eyes behind lightly tinted glasses and dark slicked-back hair. Frank thought his hair might be tied back in a ponytail. It was hard to tell from the picture, though.

Frank handed the magazine back to his brother when the light changed, and Joe picked up where he had left off. " 'Zall has been the driving force behind the hit series 'The Andersons' for five years,' " he read.

Frank had never watched the program, but the name was familiar. "Isn't that the cartoon show about the guy who writes cartoon shows for a living?''

"Right," Joe said. "Except when you see his cartoons, they're not cartoons at all—they're real people."

"And his name is Anderson?" Frank asked.

"No, his name is Herbert Swizzlestick."

"Then why is the show called 'The Andersons'?"

"That's the name of Swizzlestick's cartoon show," Joe answered.

"The one where the cartoons aren't cartoons?"

"Right," Joe said, and he chuckled to himself.

"What's so funny?" Frank asked.

"I was just remembering this episode where Swizzlestick wakes up one day and finds himself in the Andersons' world—except he's not awake, he's really asleep, and it's all a dream."

Frank shot a sidelong glance at his brother. "Do you watch this show often?"

"Hardly at all anymore," Joe replied.

"That's a relief," Frank said. "It's nice to know you're finally outgrowing cartoons."

"I'm not," Joe said bluntly. "It's just that all the good ones are on Saturday morning before nine. Who's up that early on weekends?"

"I'm glad we're almost home," Frank muttered. "I don't think I could take much more of this conversation."

When they got home, Frank headed straight for his computer, hooked it up to the telephone modem, and started typing. A list of names and numbers flashed on the computer screen.

Frank scanned the list and tapped some more keys.

Somewhere a thousand miles away another computer answered the phone and connected Frank's computer to a nationwide data base. It zapped the responses to Frank's questions through telephone lines at the speed of light. "Ah." Frank sighed with satisfaction as the computer screen lit up with information. "I just love technology."

"And I'd just love to know what you're doing," Joe said over his shoulder.

"There are businesses that make it their business to know how well other businesses are doing," Frank said.

"If you say so," Joe responded doubtfully.

"I'm linked up to a computer data base that is giving me a complete rundown on Tadd, Zall, Falk Productions," Frank explained.

"Will it tell you where Bert Zall was the night of the fire?"

"No, but it might reveal a clue about possible motives."

"I thought we already had a motive. Zall doesn't want Andrea's cartoon show competing with his."

"That isn't enough," Frank argued. "His show has been on for five years, and it's a big hit. Why would he suddenly start to panic over a little competition from a show nobody has even seen yet?"

"Good question," Joe said. "What does the computer say?"

Frank studied the screen and frowned. "Nothing very useful. There's only minimal financial information. Based on these numbers, it would appear that Tadd, Zall, Falk Productions is making tons of money—but that's just the surface picture."

"Then we need to dig beneath the surface," Joe said.

Frank turned off the computer and disconnected the modem. "I want to follow up some other leads first." He picked up the phone and punched in a local number.

"Bayport Motel," a woman's friendly voice announced on the other end of the line. "How may I help you?"

"Do you have a guest named Lynn St. Pierre registered?" Frank asked.

"Hold on," the perky voice said. "I'll check."

Frank heard a faint click and then a ringing tone. "I didn't want her to put the call through," he muttered.

"Hello? Hello?" He heard Lynn's voice in the receiver as he hung up the phone.

"That wasn't very polite," Joe said. "How did you know she was staying at the Bayport Motel?"

"It was an educated guess," Frank replied. "Her rented house is a pile of rubble, and that motel is nearby."

"Why did you hang up on her?" Joe asked.

"I didn't want her to know we were coming," Frank said.

"I didn't know we were going."

"Now you do."

"We're here to see Lynn St. Pierre," Frank told the smiling young woman behind the counter.

"I'll ring her room and see if she's in," the desk clerk said cheerfully.

She picked up the house phone and dialed a number, waited thirty seconds or so, and then hung up. "I'm sorry," she said, still smiling. "Ms. St. Pierre doesn't answer. Would you like to leave a message?"

"I just talked to her on the phone a few minutes ago," Frank said, stretching the truth. "If she left, you would have seen her go out."

"She'd be hard to miss," Joe added. "She's just a little shorter than a flagpole, and her hair doesn't quite glow in the dark."

The desk clerk's smile grew even wider, if that was possible. "Oh, you mean that tall, red-headed woman. She went into the coffee shop. It's right down the hall on the left."

Joe easily spotted Lynn's crop of flame red hair from the entrance of the coffee shop. He started to march right up to her booth, but Frank grabbed his arm and jerked him back.

"There's somebody with her," Frank whispered.

85

Joe craned his neck to get a better view of the booth. "Anybody we know?"

"Not personally," Frank murmured. "Only by reputation."

Joe's eyes widened when Lynn moved her head. His gaze fell on a man with tinted glasses and dark, slicked-back hair tied in a ponytail. "That's Bert Zall!" he exclaimed.

Chapter

10

FRANK CLAMPED A HAND over his brother's mouth and yanked him back out into the corridor. "Why don't you get a megaphone?" he whispered. "Then you wouldn't have to shout so loud!"

"I wasn't *that* loud," Joe protested in a low voice.

"I just hope Lynn didn't hear you," Frank said. "I don't want her to know that we know who Zall is."

Joe understood perfectly. Sometimes people had looser lips when they thought they were just talking to a couple of dumb teenagers. The less Frank and Joe revealed about themselves, the more they might learn from Lynn St. Pierre.

The Hardys strolled calmly back into the coffee shop and casually ambled by the booth where Lynn St. Pierre and Bert Zall were sitting.

"Frank?" Lynn called out as they passed. "Joe?"

"Oh, hi, Lynn," Frank said, acting surprised.

"Hi, I'm Joe Hardy," Joe said, extending his hand to Bert Zall.

Bert Zall smiled thinly and sat there with his hands folded on the table. The cold eyes behind the tinted lenses flicked between the two brothers. "I was just leaving," he said as he stood up and grabbed a leather overcoat off the wide seat. He buttoned the coat with precise, crisp movements and then turned to Lynn. "Good luck with the show," he said tersely.

"I don't think he really meant that," Joe said, watching Zall leave the coffee shop. "Mind if we join you?" he asked Lynn as he slid into the booth.

"Not at all," Lynn said. "A couple of friendly faces would be a welcome relief."

"I hope we didn't interrupt anything important," Frank said.

Lynn shrugged. "Bert Zall thinks everybody in the animation business should either work for him or not work at all."

"Did you ever work for him?" Joe asked.

"No," she replied, "and I probably never will. I said no to him. Not many people do, and he doesn't like it.

"When Skip and I first came up with the concept for 'Rex Rover,' " she continued, "we took it to Zall."

"And he turned you down?" Joe ventured.

"We turned *him* down," Lynn said. "He loved the idea so much he wanted to own it. He tried to buy all the rights from us. But we weren't selling; we were only looking for a producer. And I'm not about to abandon my creation now just because some hotshot like Zall waves a wad of money in my face."

Joe frowned slightly. "I don't understand. Why did he think you'd change your mind and sell him the rights now?"

"He didn't offer to buy 'Rex Rover,' " Lynn explained. "He offered me a job working on another cartoon show."

"Could you sell the rights if you wanted?" Frank asked.

"With a lot of legal footwork I could probably sell my half," Lynn answered.

"What about Skip Guzman's share?" Frank pressed. "What happens to that now?"

Lynn cocked her head at him. "You sure ask some strange questions. Why do you want to know?"

Frank was caught off guard. He had steered the conversation toward this one question. The answer was important—but he couldn't let Lynn know that.

"Frank's interested in law," Joe spoke up, covering for his brother. "He's already looking at college catalogs for schools that have good pre-law programs."

Lynn smiled. "I should have guessed. He looks like the lawyer type."

Frank cleared his throat. "Let's see if I've got this straight. You and Skip were fifty-fifty partners. But now that he's dead, you don't have a partner anymore."

"It would take a pretty sloppy lawyer to write a contract that didn't cover that contingency," Lynn told him. "Skip's share goes into a trust fund for his daughter."

"His daughter?" Frank asked.

"She lives in California with her mother. They had Skip's body flown out there for the funeral." Lynn shuddered. "We've decided to have a memorial service for him here in a couple of weeks. In the meantime I intend to make sure that Laura's half makes her very wealthy."

"How are you going to do that?" Joe asked.

"By writing great scripts and making 'Rex Rover' a megahit," Lynn declared with conviction.

In between homework, sleep, and school the next day, Frank spent his spare time thinking about the case and what to do next. Since Lynn St. Pierre had nothing to gain from Skip Guzman's death and apparently had a lot to lose if 'Rex Rover' wasn't successful, Frank finally had to admit that she made a lousy suspect.

"So what's the plan?" Joe asked as they climbed into the van after school.

"We don't have enough to go on," Frank complained. "We need a few solid leads."

"I've got an idea," Joe said. "Let's go out to the farm and look for more clues."

Frank glanced at his brother. "That's kind of a long shot at this point. The police have already gone over that area, and so have we."

"I know," Joe replied. "But Vanessa asked me to come out to the house."

Frank raised his eyebrows. "Oh? Are you sure you want me tagging along?"

Joe grinned. "You might as well. I mean, it's not as if Vanessa and I will be alone or anything. Her mother and a dozen other people will be there working on the show."

"That's true," Frank said. "Maybe we can find out something from one of them."

Joe knew that was a long shot, too, but he didn't say anything.

When they walked into the old farmhouse Frank was almost overwhelmed by the number of computers and electronic gizmos crammed into the house.

The cramped space was definitely chaotic, too. A guy with long, straggly hair zipped by in a wheeled desk chair, scooting from one computer terminal to another. He almost collided with the woman who was impatiently yanking paper out of a printer one sheet at a time.

Andrea Bender waved from across the room and called out to the Hardys. "There's no space down here for any more bodies! You'll find Vanessa upstairs!''

To Joe, Vanessa's room looked like a miniature version of her mother's setup downstairs. A large "desk" thrown together from two small filing cabinets and a wide slab of plywood took up about a third of the space. The surface of the desk was crowded with computer equipment and loose diskettes. The centerpiece was an impressive large-screen monitor.

"Let's get photographic evidence of this mess," Joe kidded Vanessa, picking up an instant camera from her desk and aiming it at her.

Vanessa smiled mischievously. "I've got a better idea," she said, snatching the camera out of his hands. She stepped way back, pointed it at him, and clicked the shutter before he realized what she was doing.

The electronic flash flared in Joe's face, and all he could see for the next few seconds were angry red dots dancing in front of his eyes. He heard the whine of the camera spitting out the picture and managed to get his vision back in time to see his own startled image appear on the glossy photo paper.

"I look deranged," Joe muttered.

"It'll make a great mug shot for an FBI most-wanted poster," Frank said.

Vanessa held the snapshot at arm's length. "It'll do," she said, lifting the lid of a box-shaped machine and placing the photograph on a flat, clear glass surface.

"Don't tell me you're going to make copies of it," Joe groaned.

"Okay, I won't," Vanessa replied. "This isn't a photocopier—it's a digital scanner. It's converting the picture into a digitized image." She sat down at the computer keyboard and hit a few keys. "And I can make that image do all kinds of things."

The wild-eyed picture of Joe suddenly filled the large computer screen.

"Can you make it disappear?" Joe asked hopefully.

"That wouldn't be any fun," Vanessa said. "But I *will* get rid of the background."

Using a penlike stylus that was wired to the computer, Vanessa worked on a flat pad beside the monitor. On the computer screen a thin black line appeared and snaked around the contours of Joe's head and body. When the outline was complete, Vanessa tapped some more keys, and her room disappeared from behind the image on the screen.

"That's better," she said. "Now he has room to move."

"You'll have to give him some feet first," Frank observed. "The photograph cut him off at the ankles."

"No problem." Vanessa moved the stylus on the pad again, and a pair of huge red clown shoes grew out of the bottoms of Joe's legs.

"Very funny," Joe mumbled.

"We haven't even gotten to the really good

part yet," Vanessa said, oblivious to Joe's reaction.

Joe watched as she cut the legs off his computerized image. Then she cut them in half again at the knees. Her right hand jumped back and forth between the pen-shaped stylus and the keyboard as she swiveled the leg parts around. She always made sure that the top and bottom halves of each leg remained connected at the knee joint and that the thigh touched the body at the hip. Then she did the same thing with the arms.

"I'm teaching the computer a set of movements," she explained as she worked. "There, that should do it." She pressed one final key combination and leaned back in her chair.

Joe's image did a clumsy dance and shuffled across the screen like a puppet on a string.

Vanessa beamed at Joe. "What do you think? Let me take a couple more pictures of you from the side and back and we can make a three-D image. Then we can rotate it and make it do just about anything."

"That's incredible," Joe said as he watched the computer screen. "I have to admit I'm really impressed."

"I'd like to see it in three-D," Frank said.

"It'll take a little while," Vanessa replied. She glanced around the room. "We need better light—and a solid white background would make it easier."

Frank looked out the window. "How about

the backyard? There's still some sunlight, and the field is covered with snow.''

"Perfect," Vanessa said, jumping up and grabbing the camera. "Let's do it."

Frank and Joe followed Vanessa downstairs through what had been a kitchen and out the back door. Vanessa told Joe to stand facing first one way, then the other, and she finally asked him to turn his back to the camera. When Vanessa decided she had enough pictures they headed back to the house.

"Wait a minute," Joe said on the back porch. He yanked the camera out of Vanessa's grasp and raised it to eye level. "If I'm going to be a computerized geek, I'm not going to be alone."

He centered her face in the viewfinder and pressed the shutter button. The electronic flash made a popping noise and banished the late-afternoon shadows with a sheet of white light. Suddenly the window behind Vanessa's head exploded into a thousand shards of glass.

Joe jerked the camera away from his face, and Vanessa whirled around at the sound of the window shattering. Joe heard the popping noise again, as something smashed into the back door with a dull thud, sending splinters flying in the air.

"Get down!" Frank screamed. "Those are gunshots!"

Chapter

11

JOE GRABBED VANESSA and dived for the floor. Frank had ducked behind a post, and Joe realized that he and Vanessa were out in the open, directly in the line of fire.

"Come on!" he urged in a tense whisper, tugging on Vanessa's arm and crawling for cover behind another post. It was only a few feet away, but it felt like a hundred miles. Joe strained to hear every sound. If he heard the lethal popping noise from a gunshot again, he planned to hurl himself on top of Vanessa and shield her with his body.

"Can you see anything?" he called out to Frank when he and Vanessa were safely huddled behind the post.

Frank peered around one side of the wood col-

umn and then around the other. The air was omi-
nously still. The field was clear, and there was
no movement in the forest beyond it. "Nothing
from here!" he called back. "Are you guys
okay?"

Joe looked at Vanessa. She gave him a nervous nod. "Yes," Joe told his brother.

Joe heard the faint sound of a car starting deep
in the woods. "Stay here!" he ordered Vanessa
as he leapt to his feet and vaulted over the porch
railing.

"Come back here!" Frank shouted, with no
hope that Joe would listen. "Don't move," he
warned Vanessa as he bounded off the porch
and took off after his brother.

Joe zigzagged across the field, crouching low
and keeping a sharp eye on the shadows in the
woods. He was pretty sure the shooter wasn't
out there anymore, but he didn't want to press
his luck. He didn't have to look back to know
that Frank was right behind him. Frank wouldn't
let Joe go out there alone.

Frank didn't know if he should be furious with
Joe or with himself. Running unarmed across an
open field toward a hidden, gun-wielding enemy
was madness, Frank knew. Yet there he was
doing it.

Joe darted into the forest and headed for the
access road. He doubted that he would reach
the road in time, but he was determined to give
it his best shot. He poured on a burst of speed,
leaping over fallen tree trunks and bulldozing

through snow-covered bushes, scattering the white powder like dust.

"Wait up!" Frank shouted as he vainly tried to catch up with his brother.

Joe was pumping so hard when he hit the narrow, rutted track that he almost ran across it and into the trees on the far side. He skidded to a stop and looked up and down the old access road. There was just a hint of exhaust fumes in the crisp air, but the car had disappeared. Joe knew it was long gone. Exhausted, he bent over and put his hands on his knees to try to catch his breath.

Frank stood with his hands on his hips, sucking in long, deep breaths of cold air and blowing out plumes of steam. He watched in silence as his brother trudged heavily back toward him. The frustration on Joe's face told him that the shooter had made a clean getaway.

The fresh tire tracks told him what he already suspected. "This is the same pattern we took a mold of," he told Joe. "Whoever fired those shots has been here before."

"Maybe we should stake out this spot," Joe suggested halfheartedly. He knew the culprit wouldn't return to the scene a third time.

They found the gunman's footprints in the snow and traced them back to a spot at the edge of the woods. "He was shooting from a prone position," Frank said, sweeping his arm across a six-foot depression in the snow. "And he rested the barrel of the rifle on this rock for extra stability."

"As easy as shooting ducks in a barrel," Joe remarked grimly.

"Yes," Frank said in a slow, distracted voice. "It was." He crouched down and sighted along the top of the rock. He had a clear view of the back porch less than thirty yards away. "So how could he miss—and who was he aiming for?"

"He could have mistaken Vanessa for her mother," Joe said. "They look a lot alike."

Frank frowned. "From this distance? He'd have to have pretty bad eyesight."

"That could explain why he missed," Joe pointed out.

Just then three Bayport police cars pulled into the driveway, sirens wailing and blue lights strobing. Frank and Joe jogged back to the house as Vanessa came out, followed closely by her mother.

"Are you guys all right?" Vanessa asked. Joe thought she sounded more angry than worried. She confirmed his perception by kicking him in the shin.

"Ow!" he yelped. "What did you do that for?"

"That's for being a macho moron!" she snapped. "What did you expect me to do after you took off and left me—huddle out in the cold and wait to see if you came back with or without a new hole in your head?"

"Well, I—" Joe began.

"I'll tell you what I did," she cut him off. "I got up, went to the nearest phone, and called the police."

"It's nice to know that somebody was thinking clearly," a stern voice behind the Hardys intoned. It was the voice of Officer Con Riley.

Joe looked down at the ground. "I almost had him," he said sullenly.

"Let's take it from the beginning," Riley said calmly. "Tell me the whole story."

Frank and Joe took turns relating everything that had happened. When they showed Con the sniper's spot at the edge of the woods, Vanessa and her mother came along, too.

"Let's not jump to any conclusions," Riley said after studying the area of flattened snow. "A sleeping deer could have made this impression. There are deer tracks all around here."

"A deer with a high-powered rifle?" Frank countered.

"As I recall," Riley said, "we've gotten several complaints from Ms. Bender about poachers in these woods."

"Nobody ever shot at us before," Andrea Bender said, an edge to her voice.

"It could have been an accident," the police officer said. "Stray shots from a careless hunter who panicked and ran when he realized what he had done."

"Is that what you're going to put in your report?" Joe asked sharply.

"You know me better than that," Riley responded evenly. "My report will include your version of what might have happened. It will also cover the other possibilities."

"Sounds fair to me," Frank said before Joe could argue.

Lynn St. Pierre was waiting for them back inside the house. "You gave me quite a scare," she told Vanessa. "I was having a relatively normal phone conference with your mother when you burst onto the line, screaming about a shooting. I had to get in my car and come straight over."

She turned to Vanessa's mother. "Is everybody okay?"

"Everything's fine now," Vanessa said. "Nobody got hurt."

"Everything is *not* fine!" Andrea Bender snapped. "You could have been killed!"

Vanessa gave her mother a stunned look. "You make it sound like it was my fault!"

The hard lines on Andrea's face softened. "I'm sorry, kiddo," she said softly. "I didn't mean to bark at you. I feel like we're under some kind of curse. Why are all these horrible things happening?"

Frank looked at Lynn. "You told us Bert Zall wanted to buy the rights to 'Rex Rover.' Do you think he'd go this far to stop the show from going on the air?"

"You mean hire a hit man?" Lynn responded. "I doubt it. Zall doesn't need to resort to violence. He just buys whatever or whoever he wants."

"He couldn't buy you," Joe reminded her.

"So there are a few exceptions," Lynn said.

"Too few," Andrea said bitterly.

"What do you mean?" Frank asked.

Andrea sat down heavily in the nearest chair and sighed. "I mean, Bert Zall has been a busy little beaver the last few days. He hired away one of my best colorists, and I doubt he'll be the last."

"Can't you hire another colorist to replace him?" Joe responded.

"It's not that simple," Andrea explained. "It would take time to train a replacement—and time is one thing I don't have."

"Maybe you can get an extension on the deadline from the television network," Frank suggested.

Lynn let out a low, bitter chuckle. "You obviously don't know Pete Moss, the head of programming. He wouldn't give his own mother an extension."

"Lynn's right," Andrea said wearily. "If Zall keeps hiring away my people, there's no way I'll be able to make the deadline for the first episode."

Chapter

12

"Do you think Zall is trying to drive you out of business?" Frank asked.

"I wouldn't put it past him," Andrea said. "He's done it to others."

Joe tugged on Vanessa's sleeve and pulled her off to the side. "Can you get me the name, phone number, and address of the colorist who quit here to work for Zall?"

Vanessa nodded. "I think so. I'll call you later and let you know."

By the time Frank and Joe got home Joe was almost too tired to eat. All the events of the long week were starting to take their toll. After dinner he trudged up to his room, flopped down on his bed to rest for a little while, and was soon fast asleep.

The phone rang, jolting him awake. He squinted against a harsh light coming from somewhere, fumbled for the receiver, and managed to get one end close to his ear.

"Wha? Who?" he mumbled.

"Joe?" Vanessa's voice came through the phone. "Did I wake you? I'm sorry. I know it's early."

"Early?" Joe echoed, sitting up and squinting one bleary eye at the clock. The digital readout said eight-fifteen and the bright sun streaming in the window told him it wasn't eight-fifteen at night.

"What day is it?" he asked cautiously.

"Saturday," Vanessa said in a puzzled voice.

"That's a relief," Joe said. "For a second there I thought I was going to be late for school." Then he remembered what he had asked Vanessa to do. "Did you find out the name of the colorist?"

"His name is Josh Barr," Vanessa told him. "He lives in Woodston."

"Woodston?" Joe responded. "That's over seventy miles from here."

"My mom uses a lot of free-lance talent," Vanessa explained. "Josh works at home. He drives into Bayport only once a week to drop off painted animation cels and pick up a new batch."

Vanessa gave Joe the colorist's phone number, and he started dialing right after he said goodbye to her. Joe's conversation with Josh Barr was short and direct. Barr told Joe that Zall had made him a very generous offer that he simply couldn't pass up. Joe asked a few more questions and jotted down some information in a small notebook.

After talking to Barr Joe dialed another number, listened to a recorded message, and hung up. Then he got dressed and went to look for his brother.

"I figured you'd be here," Joe said when he found Frank hunched over his computer.

"You're just in time," Frank said, pointing at the screen.

Joe peered at the monitor and saw a bunch of dollar signs, numbers, and words like *capital investment, operating expenses,* and *net revenues.*

"I knew it," he muttered. "You've decided to give up the detective business and become an accountant."

Frank ignored Joe's comment. "I was trying to get more information about Zall's company, but I came up empty. But since I was already linked up to the nationwide business data base, I decided to poke around and see what I could find out about Gem Graphics."

"Phil Gemowski's company," Joe stated, now staring at the screen with renewed interest. "So what do all these numbers mean?"

"If you look at the recent data alone," Frank replied, "the company doesn't seem to be in very bad shape. But if you go back a few years, you can see there's a definite downhill trend. My guess is that it started around the time Andrea left to start her own company."

"I told you we should check out Gemowski," Joe said.

"We will," Frank assured him, "right after we follow up on Zall."

"That reminds me," Joe said. "I talked to the colorist Zall stole. He told me that Zall asked him for the phone number of another colorist, a guy named Stephen Hickey.

"Hickey just moved to Bayport," Joe continued. "I tried his number and got a telephone company recording. Hickey's phone hasn't been connected yet."

"We should try again later," Frank said.

"In the meantime," Joe said, "why don't we swing by the Benders' place?"

Frank couldn't help grinning. "It's been over fifteen hours since you last saw Vanessa. I think that's the longest you've been apart since you met her."

Joe's face flushed. "I just thought we should check up on them, make sure they're okay. That's all. Forget it. We don't have to go."

"Actually," Frank said casually, "I was thinking about driving out to the farm anyway. There's a question that I want to ask Vanessa."

"What's that?" Joe asked warily.

Frank's grin widened. "What does she see in you?"

The sun was no longer shining when Frank and Joe climbed into the van. Thick gray clouds had moved in, filling the sky, and a light snow began to fall as Frank backed the van out the driveway. A storm had begun by the time Joe hopped out of the van at the farmhouse. There was almost an inch of new snow on the ground and more coming down at a furious pace.,

Joe was glad to get out of the bitter cold, and he was glad to see Vanessa again.

"I'm just finishing up the animated three-D version of you," Vanessa explained as the image of Joe slowly rotated on the screen. "I took those photographs of you and ran them through the digitizer, then fed all the data into the three-D program.

"First," she continued as she tapped on the keyboard, "I used the basic contours to make a wire model." Joe saw a grid of curved, criss-crossed lines, shaped like a body, replace the revolving image of himself on the computer monitor. "Then I molded your features onto the frame." Joe's face appeared on the screen and wrapped itself around the wire-frame head. Then hair sprouted on top, followed by clothes, hands, and finally feet.

"That's amazing," Joe said. "What can it do besides spin like a chicken on a barbecue rack?"

"I'm working on that now," Vanessa said. "It takes a long time to make the body movements look smooth and natural. I start with some basic positions, like sitting and standing, and then the computer helps me with the in-between steps."

The video version of Joe stood up and sat down in an invisible chair over and over again.

"How long will it take for you to program it to take out the garbage?" Frank quipped. "Our parents have been trying for seventeen years. He still doesn't do it."

They all laughed as the little Joe on the screen kept sitting down and standing up.

"Hey, I've got an idea," Joe said. "Can you stop it halfway between the sitting and standing positions?"

"Sure," Vanessa replied. She pressed a few keys and the image shifted into slow motion. "Just say when."

"Right there," Joe said.

The figure froze in an awkward crouch.

"Now move the arms out to the sides."

"Like this?" Vanessa asked.

"Perfect," Joe said. "Now show me how to use that drawing gizmo."

Vanessa gave him a quick lesson on how to use the electronic stylus and pad. Joe drew a crude oval shape beneath the feet of the figure and sketched a triangle jutting out from the underside of the long oval.

"Okay," Joe finally said. "We're ready to roll. Can you make the whole thing go across the screen like this?" he asked, tracing a pattern in the air with his finger.

"That's easy," Vanessa answered. She moved the image to a few different places on the screen, tapping a few keys at each spot. "Lights, camera, action!" she declared as she pressed one final key and sat back.

The crouching image of Joe bobbed up and down across the screen in steep curves.

"Look!" Joe exclaimed with delight. "I'm surfing!"

While Joe and Vanessa were engrossed in Joe's animated antics, Frank slipped out of the room and found a telephone in the hall. This time there was an answer when he dialed Stephen Hickey's number. "I don't know any other way to put this," he said after he had introduced himself to the colorist and explained a little about the case, "so I'll just ask you straight out."

"Let me guess," the voice on the other end said. "You want to know if Bert Zall has contacted me, right?"

"I guess that means he has," Frank said.

Hickey chuckled. "As soon as I plugged in the phone it started ringing. Zall must have one of those computerized call-back systems that constantly dials a number until somebody answers.

"You can tell Andrea to relax," he continued. "I don't want to work for Bert Zall, but I'm having a little trouble ramming that idea into his thick skull."

"What do you mean?" Frank asked.

"Even though I already gave him a definite no, he still wants to stop by here late this afternoon to give me his sales pitch in person. I think I'll just call his office and tell him I won't be here."

"Do me a favor," Frank said. "Don't make that call."

Frank was hanging up when Joe and Vanessa came out of her room.

"There you are," Joe said. "Come on. We're going outside to build a snowman. He's going to be the star of our surfing cartoon."

"A surfing snowman?" Frank wondered.

Vanessa smiled. "Why not? Anything's possible in animation."

Several inches of new snow had piled up on the roof of the van while Frank and Joe were in the house. A few big wet flakes were still drifting down, but the worst of it was mostly over. Vanessa scooped up a snowball and threw it at Joe, hitting him in the back of the head. He whirled around and fired one back. Vanessa ducked, and Frank got a face full of snow.

"I think I'll just go sit in the van," Frank said as he wiped his eyes clear. "You kids go ahead and play in the snow."

"Walk down to the mailbox with me," Vanessa said, taking Joe's hand. "I want to see if the new issue of *Animation News* came today."

A boxy black Jeep with studded snow tires and a snowplow rig on the front rolled into the long driveway as Joe and Vanessa trudged down to the mailbox.

"I was wondering who had to shovel this thing," Joe remarked.

"My mom pays some guy a monthly fee to plow the driveway whenever it snows," Vanessa explained. "Usually we have to get at least six inches before he'll show up. I didn't expect to see him today." She paused and stared at the jeep. "That's funny. I thought he had a truck."

The jeep stopped, and Joe eyed it warily. Gears clanked and an electric motor whined as the plow blade sank down into the snow. Then the engine roared, and the jeep lurched forward.

"He seems to be in a bit of a hurry today," Joe said nervously, grabbing Vanessa's arm and pulling her off the driveway and out of the plow's path.

Joe's eyes widened as the machine hurtled up the driveway, churning snow and gravel. Then suddenly the Jeep swerved off the driveway and bore down on Joe and Vanessa, picking up speed as the gleaming metal plow blade chewed up the short distance to its target.

Chapter
13

"RUN!" JOE SHOUTED, and he sprinted away from the driveway, yanking Vanessa with him. The jeep pursued them, the steel blade on the front carving an angry white furrow in the open field. Joe was desperate to find cover of any kind.

"He's right behind us!" Vanessa screamed. "What should we do?"

Joe dragged her toward the trees. Even though he knew they were too far, he had to try for their cover. It was their only chance.

Joe could hear the plow blade slicing through the snow and scraping over rocks. He didn't dare look back. He did catch sight of something out of the corner of his eye and on an impulse grasped Vanessa's hand with both of his and whipped her around in a forceful arc. When he let go Vaneesa sailed across the snow, windmilling her arms as she corkscrewed through the air. She came down on her back—and was almost completely swallowed up by a deep snowdrift.

Joe hurled himself after her like a long jumper going for the world record. He landed on his feet and sank like a stone, buried up to his waist in the three-foot drift. Joe held his breath. Either he had just saved their lives or he had killed them both.

The black Jeep plowed straight at them but ground to a halt at the drift. The snow was too heavy and deep for the blade to slice through. The blade was close enough that Joe could have reached out and touched it, but it wouldn't get to him across the mound of snow.

Joe could only see the driver's eyes through the eyeholes of the dark ski mask as the jeep was slammed into reverse. The tires spun wildly, and the Jeep lurched backward. It skidded and slid all the way back to the driveway, turned around, and tore off down the open road.

Frank ran across the field as Joe and Vanessa waded out of the drift. "Are you guys okay? I called the police on the car phone," he told them. "I gave them a description of the vehicle. Did you see the license plate?"

Joe shook his head and dusted snow off his pants. "All I saw was that big, ugly snowplow blade."

"What about the driver?" Frank asked hopefully.

"I got a great close-up look at him." Joe said. "I don't think I'd have much trouble picking out his dark blue ski mask in a police lineup. So if we just round up everybody in the state who owns a blue ski mask, we're bound to find our man."

"Or woman," Vanessa added. "Who could tell with that mask on?"

Frank studied the ground around them. "We may not know who it is," he said, nodding at the tread pattern in the snow, "but this isn't the first time our paths have crossed."

Ten minutes later the police arrived. Con Riley took one look at the path in the field and sealed off the area.

"This was definitely not an accident," he told Vanessa's mother.

"Gee, really?" Joe responded bitterly. "How do you know the driver didn't just lose control of the vehicle and dig up forty yards of the field trying to stop?"

"Don't pay any attention to him," Frank told his friend. "The important thing now is to find the person who did this."

"We put out a bulletin on the vehicle," Riley replied. "There can't be too many black Jeeps equipped with snowplows. But if the guy keeps the car off the street or takes off the plow, we're not likely to find him."

"What about the tracks?" Vanessa asked.

"Can't you match the tread pattern to the car's tires?"

"Sure—once we have a possibility they'll be important. We can't use the tracks to find the vehicle. They're only good for confirming we've found the right one."

Andrea Bender stared numbly at the police officer. "Are you saying you can't do anything about this?"

"We're doing everything we can," Riley said gently. "If we had more to go on, we'd do more."

"Then we'll just have to get you more," Joe said flatly.

Joe had nobody but himself to blame when he found himself sitting in the van several hours later, staring at an apartment building down the street.

"I hate stakeouts," Joe grumbled as he restlessly drummed his fingers on the van's steering wheel. He glanced at the clock on the dashboard. "It's almost four. Is this 'late' afternoon?"

Frank gave a casual shrug, keeping a watchful eye on the apartment building. "It all depends on your point of view. I might think it's late, and you might think it's late—but if Bert Zall doesn't think it's late, then it's not late."

"When did we change over to Zall time?" Joe responded.

"When we decided to stake out this place and

wait for him. He told Stephen Hickey he'd stop by his apartment late this afternoon.''

"And Hickey told you he wasn't going to be there when Zall showed up.''

"But Zall doesn't know that," Frank said.

"Do you think Zall's our man?" Joe asked.

"It's possible," Frank said without committing himself. "Right now we're a little low on suspects."

"That's true," Joe acknowledged. "Lynn St. Pierre doesn't have a motive. Akira Fukojima has an alibi and the wrong tires. And after two murder attempts on her daughter, I'd say Andrea Bender is definitely out of the running.''

"I've been thinking about that," Frank said pensively. "Why did the killer go after Vanessa? Twenty-four hours ago I was willing to consider the possibility that the shooting incident might have been a case of mistaken identity. But after what happened this morning it just doesn't hold up anymore."

"Maybe he's after you and me," Joe ventured. "We were both on the porch yesterday when the lead started flying, and that snowplow would have iced me along with Vanessa."

"Possible," Frank replied quietly. "Somebody could be trying to scare us off the case. That would also explain the incident with the rock that hit the van." He turned the idea over in his mind. "Then whoever it is has to be someone who knows we're on the case."

"We haven't exactly made a secret of it," Joe pointed out.

"We haven't rented any billboards, either," Frank countered.

Joe stopped drumming on the steering wheel and focused out the window. "I do believe Mr. Zall has arrived," Joe said as if announcing him.

A white limousine pulled up in front of the apartment building. The back door opened, and a man in a full-length leather coat got out. His long dark hair was slicked back and tied in a ponytail.

"Nice car," Frank said. "Too bad it's not a black Jeep."

Joe looked at his brother. "We didn't hang around here all this time just to see what kind of car Zall drives, did we?"

"No," Frank answered, opening his door. "But it would have made our job a lot easier."

They found Zall in the lobby of the apartment building, scanning the rows of mailboxes, each with a nameplate and a buzzer above it.

"Don't bother," Joe said, startling the man. "He's not home."

"I beg your pardon?" the man with the pony-tail responded, turning his sharp gaze on the Hardys.

"The man you want to buy doesn't want to be bought," Joe told him.

Zall cocked his head to one side. "Do I know you from somewhere?"

"I realize you're a busy man," Frank said in

117

a pleasant tone, smiling and stepping on his brother's foot. "We'd like to ask you a few questions. It'll only take a minute or two."

"I remember now," the man said. "You were in the coffee shop. You're Lynn's friends, right? Did she put you up to this?"

"Nobody put us up to anything," Joe snapped. "In case you hadn't heard, a man was murdered. We want to make sure nobody else gets hurt."

Zall laughed. The sound was hard and brittle. "I get it. You're Andrea Bender's idea of hired muscle. What are you going to do? Beat me up? Well, before you do, I suggest you look behind you."

Joe glanced back over his shoulder and saw a human wall in a chauffeur's outfit. The cap perched on the man's huge head was almost comical, but there was nothing funny about the thick mass of muscles bulging at the seams of the uniform.

"Very impressive," Frank said calmly. "Did he come with the limo, or did you have to pay extra for him?"

"Nothing's free," Zall replied. "You have to pay for everything in this world."

"And everbody has a price," Joe said harshly. "Right?"

A cold, thin smile appeared on the man's face. "Most people do. What's yours?"

"Higher than you can afford," Joe replied, locking his unblinking eyes on Zall's. "And if anything happens to Andrea or Vanessa Bender, I'll make sure you pay in full."

Zall laughed again. The sound was just as unpleasant as before. "So that's it. You think I had something to do with the fire that killed Skip Guzman? Interesting idea—but you're threatening the wrong producer."

"What do you mean?" Frank asked.

"Andrea should choose her friends more carefully," Zall responded. "Rumor has it that one of them went behind her back and cut a secret deal with the network."

Joe frowned. "What kind of deal?"

"I'm not sure," Zall said. "Why don't you ask Slick Gemowski?"

Frank stared at the man. "Slick?"

"An old nickname of Phil's that he never liked much," Zall explained. "I guess nobody calls him that anymore." He climbed into his limo.

Something clicked in Frank's head as the chauffeur took off. "Slick Gemowski," he repeated, turning to his brother.

Joe suddenly realized why the nickname was important. "S. G.," he said in a stunned voice. "The initials on the lighter we found in the rubble from the fire."

Chapter

14

"EVERYBODY ASSUMED those were Skip Guzman's initials on the lighter," Joe said as he started the van for the drive home. "Now that we know about Phil Gemowski's old nickname, we know that more than one S.G. is connected with this case."

"There is one small hitch, though," Frank said. "Vanessa told us that Gemowski invested in her mother's company. That's why we never considered him much of a suspect before. If Andrea loses, so does Gemowski."

"What about this secret deal with the network that Zall mentioned?" Joe responded.

"Good question," Frank said, picking up the cellular phone. "Let's see if we can find out. What was the name of the network programming guy that Lynn told us about? Was it Pete Moss?''

Joe nodded. "That sounds right."

"Well, if it isn't," Frank remarked as he punched a number into the phone, "we'll soon find out."

"Gem Graphics," a woman's crisp, voice announced on the other end of the line.

"Ah, yes," Frank replied in a deep voice. "This is Pete Moss. Put me through to Phil Gemowski."

"I'm sorry, Mr. Moss," the woman said. "Mr. Gemowski isn't in today."

"That could be a problem," Frank told her, although he was actually relieved. This would be easier if he didn't have to deal with Gemowski directly. "I need to talk to him about a certain business proposal we discussed a few weeks ago. Is there anybody else there who might be able to answer a few questions?"

"Hold on, Mr. Moss," the woman said, "I'll put you through to Mr. Gemowski's personal assistant."

"Mr. Moss?" a man's voice came on the line after a brief pause. "This is Tony Andrews. I'm sorry Phil isn't here to talk to you himself. Is there anything I can do to help?"

"That depends," Frank replied. "Do you know anything about the 'Rex Rover' project?"

"I don't know all the details, but I went over some of the projections with Phil. And let me

121

assure you that we can go into production at a moment's notice. All you have to do is give us the word."

"I see," Frank said, his mind racing. "So if Andrea Bender can't deliver on time—"

"Gem Graphics will be there to pick up the ball and run with it," Tony Andrews assured him.

"I'm sure you will," Frank said curtly. "That's all I needed to know. Thanks for your time."

"Gemowski cut a deal with the network to take over 'Rex Rover' if Andrea misses her deadline," he told Joe.

"I should have known," Joe said bitterly, cranking the steering wheel and swinging the van around in a tight U-turn.

"Whoa!" Frank exclaimed, clutching the armrest on the door. "What are you doing?"

"Going back to the farm," Joe answered. "We should tell Andrea about Gemowski's little scheme to ruin her business and steal her show."

"I have a better idea," Frank said calmly, reaching for the car phone again. "Why don't we just call her? It'd be faster than driving all the way out to the farm."

Frank dialed the Benders' number. Halfway through the first ring someone picked up on the other end.

"Yes?" a distraught voice blurted out. "What is it?"

"Who is this?" Frank asked in a puzzled tone.

"Listen," the agitated voice snapped, "I'm expecting an important call. What do you want?"

"Lynn?" Frank spoke into the phone. "Is that you? This is Frank Hardy. Could I talk to Vanessa?"

"Oh, Frank," the woman replied in a halting voice. "I'm sorry. I've been waiting for a call from Andrea. She's supposed to call me from the hospital."

"The hospital?" Frank echoed, an empty feeling in the pit of his stomach.

"Vanessa was in an accident," Lynn told him. "Her car went off the road. I don't know how bad it is. They wouldn't give Andrea any details over the phone."

Joe blasted across an intersection as the traffic light turned from yellow to red. "What happened?" he demanded sharply, gripping the wheel tightly with both hands. "How is she?"

"I don't know," Frank said. "Vanessa had a fight with her mother about something. Lynn said she stormed out of the house and took off in her car. An hour or so later Andrea got a phone call from the hospital. They told her Vanessa had been in a car crash."

"What kind of car crash?" Joe demanded, his voice high with tension. "Where did it happen?"

"We'll find out at the hospital," Frank said. "In the meantime let up on that gas pedal. The roads are icy. You won't be any help to Vanessa if you wrap the van around a tree and they have to wheel you in to see her on a stretcher."

Joe ignored the signs that pointed to the hospital parking lot and drove right up to the emergency room entrance. He slammed on the brakes, jumped out of the van, and ran into the hospital without waiting for Frank. He spotted Andrea Bender in the waiting room, hunched over in a plastic chair, holding a Styrofoam cup of coffee with both hands.

She glanced up at Joe with an expression that said she was too tired to be surprised. "How did you find out—or did you have an accident, too? There seems to be a lot of that going around."

"How's Vanessa?" Joe asked. "Is she going to be okay?"

"The doctor said there's nothing to worry about," Andrea told him. "No broken bones, no internal injuries. She should be out in a minute or two. They're giving her a few stitches where she cracked the side of her head against the window."

"Do you know what happened?" Frank's voice came from behind Joe. He was a little out of breath after running all the way from the parking lot where he had parked the van.

"She lost control of her car on a turn and smashed into a guardrail," Andrea said.

"A guardrail?" Frank responded. "Where did it happen?"

Andrea shrugged wearily. "I didn't have time to ask. She likes to drive along that road by Barmet Bay. Maybe that's where she was."

"The cliff road," Joe said. "That has guardrails on all the curves."

Joe turned to see a balding man in a baggy green surgical outfit come through a swinging double door. He held it open, and Vanessa Bender hobbled out behind him, a white gauze patch taped to the side of her head. She put on a shaky smile when she saw her mother and the Hardys.

Joe rushed over and took her arm. "Should you be walking around?" he asked, worried.

"It's no big deal," Vanessa claimed. "It wasn't even my idea to come to the emergency room. But I guess I was kind of bleeding, and the lady who picked me up sort of freaked and insisted on bringing me here."

"I'm glad she did," her mother said. "You could have been badly hurt. I've told you before, a car isn't a toy. You have to drive carefully."

"That's the weird part," Vanessa said. "I *was* driving carefully. I can't figure out how it happened. I was on that road that winds along the cliffs by the bay. I wasn't going anywhere in particular, just admiring the view. So I wasn't going too fast. But every time I went around a curve the tires squealed like those of a race car going a hundred miles an hour. Then I hit a tight turn, and the car just kind of slipped out from under me.''

''Where's the car now?'' Frank asked.

''I couldn't get it started after I smashed into the guardrail,'' Vanessa said. ''So I just left it there and started walking. That was when that lady picked me up and brought me here.''

Andrea Bender put her arm around her daughter. ''Let's get you home, kiddo.'' She looked at the Hardys. ''Could you take Vanessa back to the house? There are some things I have to do.''

Frank heard defeat in Andrea's tone, as if she had resigned herself to something unpleasant but necessary. He wanted to tell her about Phil Gemowski but decided the information could keep for a while. She was still in shock from Vanessa's accident and needed some time to recover.

After taking Vanessa home Frank and Joe drove out to the cliff road. Twenty minutes later they were standing next to Vanessa's battered car on a windswept cliff overlooking Barmet Bay and the Atlantic Ocean beyond.

Joe gazed over the edge to the turbulent blue green water below. ''Vanessa was lucky. If they hadn't reinforced these guardrails a few years ago, she might have ended up down there, under fifty feet of water.''

Frank crouched down and unscrewed the cap

from the air nozzle on the right front tire. He stuck a pressure gauge on the nozzle, checked the reading, took it off, and then put it on again to confirm the reading. He did the same with the other three tires.

"She was lucky she got this far," Frank said. "None of these tires has more than twelve pounds of pressure. That's why they squealed every time Vanessa went around a curve. Tires barely grip the road at all when the pressure's that low. Add a little snow and ice, they're worse than useless—they're dangerous."

Joe turned around and inspected one of the tires. It flattened and bulged slightly at the bottom. He pressed it with his hand, and the tire buckled inward. "I don't get it," he said. "These are brand-new tires."

Frank checked the crumpled side of the car wedged against the guardrail. "So either the guys at the service station didn't fill the tires with enough air when they put them on, or somebody deliberately let the air out because they wanted something like this to happen."

"That makes three times somebody has gone after Vanessa, not counting the day we met her when her tires had been slashed." Joe uttered the words with growing alarm. "I don't think we can wait until we find out more about Gemowski or any other suspects," he said urgently. "We'd better go to the police right now and report that somebody's trying to kill Vanessa."

*   *   *

There wasn't usually a lot of action at the Bayport police station. An occasional rowdy drunk driver was about the most excitement that came through the doors in an average week. So Frank knew something big was going on when they walked into the station and found themselves among lots of uniforms and suits.

Frank and Joe shouldered their way through the crowd and found Con Riley. "What's going on?" Frank asked.

"The chief is about to make a statement," Riley told them. "We just arrested a suspect in the Guzman murder case."

Frank stared at him, surprised. "I didn't know you were treating it as a murder case."

"We weren't," Riley said. "But Andrea Bender changed that."

Joe heard a murmur of voices in the crowd and glanced over his shoulder to see Chief Collig coming out of his office. A few flashes popped and somebody stuck a microphone in the chief's face.

"Ladies and gentlemen," the police chief announced in a loud voice, "we have a suspect in custody for the murder of Skip Guzman."

"Do you have enough evidence to prosecute?" someone shouted out.

"I believe so," Chief Collig replied. "The suspect came forth voluntarily. She's cooperating fully."

Frank and Joe looked at each other. "She?" they both whispered.

"Who is the suspect?" another voice called out.

The police chief cleared his throat and squinted as another camera flash blazed in his face. "We have a signed confession from Andrea Bender."

Chapter

15

"I DON'T BELIEVE IT," Joe said, shaking his head. "It doesn't make any sense. All the weird things that have happened the last few days are connected somehow to the fire that killed Skip Guzman, and Vanessa was the target almost every time. Why would Andrea want to hurt her own daughter?"

"And what made her decide to confess now?" Frank added.

Con Riley shrugged. "Maybe she had a guilty conscience about Guzman's death. She confessed to starting the fire but claimed she didn't know Guzman was in the studio," Con continued. "I don't know if the chief can make the murder charge stick, though."

"I knew it was her all along," a voice behind

Joe announced. He turned and saw the insurance investigator, Walt Steadman.

"She did it for the insurance money," Steadman said. "People have been killed for a lot less than five hundred grand."

"How convenient for you," Joe said bitterly. "Your company won't lose any money, and you didn't have to do any real work."

Steadman snorted. "*Real* detective work is more than just falling down and finding clues on the ground. It takes long hours of detailed research, background checks, and double-checking facts. I put a lot of time into this case. I would have nailed her sooner or later."

"So tell me something," Frank said. "Did your exhaustive research cover any suspects besides Andrea Bender?"

Steadman chuckled. "I know you boys aren't happy with the way things turned out, but don't lay the blame on me. I wasn't trying to railroad the lady. As a matter of fact, I was following up a lead on another suspect when I got word that Ms. Bender had confessed."

"Really?" Frank said casually. "Who was your other lead?"

"If you had done your homework," Steadman said smugly, "you'd know that Ms. Bender used to work for a man named Phil Gemowski."

"What a shock," Joe muttered sarcastically.

Frank kicked his brother in the shin. "What made Gemowski a suspect?" he asked the insurance investigator.

"I dug a little deeper," Steadman said proudly, "and found out that Gemowski's own animation company has been losing money recently. In fact, it's been going downhill ever since Andrea Bender left."

"I see," Frank said seriously. "So you were working on the professional jealousy angle?"

Steadman nodded and tapped the side of his head. "To catch a crook, you have to learn to think like one."

"And I'm sure you've had lots of practice," Joe said icily just before his brother dragged him out of the police station.

The Hardys drove straight to the Benders' house, where they found Vanessa in a vague state of shock.

"I know my mom didn't do it," she said desperately, clutching Joe's arm and looking at him with wide eyes. "Why did she tell the police she killed Skip? What's going on around here? Has everybody gone crazy?"

Joe put his arm around her. "Don't worry. We're not going to let your mother take the fall for this. We have a pretty good idea who the real killer is. All we need is a little more time to prove it."

Frank and Joe filled Vanessa in on what they had uncovered about Phil Gemowski. "We know he had a strong motive," Joe concluded. "But we don't have any hard evidence."

"I just remembered something about Phil Gemowski," Vanessa said. "He used to be a heavy smoker. He quit about two years ago."

"We already figured that," Frank responded. "I don't see how it will help us."

"No, you don't understand," Vanessa said urgently. "It's the way he quit smoking that's important. Every time he felt like having a cigarette he popped a stick of gum in his mouth instead. He carried two or three packs of gum around all the time. He used to joke that he would have to chew a pack of gum for every pack of cigarettes he ever smoked.

"He doesn't chew gum anymore," she added, "except when he's nervous or under a lot of pressure."

"That explains the gum wrapper we found in the woods," Joe said. "Gemowski was probably plenty nervous when he torched the studio."

"Yes," Frank agreed. "But a gum wrapper isn't enough to put Gemowski behind bars. We need more."

"What about the tire tracks?" Vanessa suggested. "You still have the mold of the tracks we found in the woods, and the police have one from the field where the black Jeep chased us."

"I'm not sure we'll be able to connect the Jeep to Gemowski very easily," Frank said. "He wasn't driving a Jeep the day we met him. He might have rented it. Even if the jeep does belong to him, he probably has it stashed somewhere safe."

Joe looked at his brother. "If? Who else could it belong to? Who else would be after Vanessa?"

"That's the part that bothers me," Frank said pensively. "Why would Gemowski go after Vanessa, and how did he manage to botch each job?"

"Gee," Vanessa said coldly, "I never considered my life a botched job before."

"I'm sorry," Frank said. "That's not what I meant. This whole case feels wrong somehow. If Gemowski wanted to get rid of your mother, he sure picked a roundabout way to do it."

A perplexed frown creased Joe's face. "You're right. It doesn't make a whole lot of sense."

"Maybe it does," Vanessa said thoughtfully. "My mom's been getting some weird phone calls lately. She never told me what any of the calls were about, but they really upset her. Then she started talking about sending me to stay with my aunt in Chicago."

"But you just moved *here*," Joe responded.

Vanessa nodded. "That's what we had the big fight about before I took off in my car and ended up in the hospital. All of a sudden she was obsessed with the idea of getting me out of town. She told me to start packing right away."

Joe frowned again. "I don't get it."

"I think I do," Frank said excitedly. "What if Gemowski wasn't really trying to kill Vanessa? What if all those attacks were only meant to scare Andrea?"

"You mean scare her into shutting down her business?" Joe ventured.

"That could have been it at first," Frank replied. "But what if he got nervous about our investigation of the fire? What if he was afraid we might turn up some evidence that would lead back to him?"

"Of course!" Joe exclaimed. "That's what the phone calls were about. Gemowski must have forced Andrea to confess by threatening to kill Vanessa."

"But why didn't she just call the police and tell them what was happening?" Vanessa responded.

"She was probably afraid he'd kill you if she contacted the police," Frank said.

"Especially if she didn't know who was making the threats. I'm sure Gemowski disguised his voice. So, if she couldn't prove anything," Joe added, "the police wouldn't have much to go on."

"It's time to turn the tables on Gemowski," Frank said, "and force him to do something that isn't part of his plan." He glanced at Vanessa and then at his brother. "I have an idea. Stand together for a minute."

"I have a bad feeling about this," Joe muttered to Vanessa as Frank eyed the two of them.

"About standing close to me?" she responded.

"No," Joe said, a little flustered. "I have a bad feeling about this idea—whatever it is."

"Oh, stop moaning," Frank said. "This is a

135

great idea. Did you know Vanessa is almost as tall as you are?''

Joe groaned. "I knew it! This is going to be another one of your plans where I have to do something stupid."

Frank grinned broadly. "Trust me. You'll love it."

"I hate this," Joe grumbled as he and Frank got into the van. He caught a glimpse of himself in the side-view mirror, and his cheeks flushed at the sight of long, curly hair. "I won't fool anybody in this wig," he complained.

"You would have looked better with the dress and makeup," Frank teased.

"The hair and Vanessa's parka are as far as I go," Joe declared. "And if anybody we know sees me in this getup, I'm going to wring your neck—with the wig."

Frank laughed. "Don't worry. We're just going for a little drive. If I'm right, Gemowski will try to keep the pressure on Vanessa for the next few days because he needs to make sure Andrea won't take back her confession. And if we're lucky, he was watching the house and saw you as Vanessa get in the van with me."

The sun had just started to set when the Hardys arrived at the farm. Now it was long gone, and night had taken over the winter sky. Frank flicked on the headlights as the van rolled away from the glare of the porch light. When he reached the road that led back to town he turned in the opposite direction, away from Bayport.

"It's a little dark out to take the scenic route," Joe remarked. "Where are we going?"

"Toward the highway," Frank answered.

"Do you really think this will work?" Joe asked.

"Gemowski has to keep a close watch on Vanessa," Frank said. "If she leaves town, he has to know where she goes. Otherwise, he doesn't have much of a hold on her mother anymore. Right?"

A pair of headlights appeared in the rearview mirror. "We've got company," Frank told his brother. "I can't tell what kind of car it is. Can you get a better look?"

"I'll give it try," Joe said, climbing into the back of the van.

There was a loud crunch, and the van suddenly lurched forward. Joe stumbled and fell on his hands and knees. "Hey!" he yelled. "What's the big idea?"

"That wasn't me!" Frank shouted. "That guy rear-ended us!"

There was another crunch. The van careened over the center line and swerved back again. Joe pitched sideways and slammed into the wall.

"He did it again!" Frank cried out.

"No kidding," Joe muttered, trying to find something to hang on to, to steady himself.

"You'd better get back up here and buckle up!" Frank urged. "This guy means business!"

Joe yanked the wig off his head and threw it on the floor. "Great plan!" he snapped. "What did you expect him to do?"

Metal clanged against metal again, sending a harsh jolt through the van. Joe clawed the air as he flew backward. His hand came down on something attached to the wall, and he clutched at it frantically. His eyes filled with horror when he felt it move and heard the ominous click of the rear door latch.

A cold blast of wind smacked Joe in the face as the door flew open, sucking him out into the night.

Chapter

16

THE VAN DOOR swung wide, and Joe clung to it, desperately gripping the door handle. His arm was almost ripped out of its socket, and a sharp pain shot all the way down to his fingertips. He gritted his teeth and held on as the pavement whizzed by at a dizzying speed beneath him.

Frank kept one eye glued to the rearview mirror, helplessly watching his brother flap around behind the van. If Frank slowed down, the car would close the gap and smash into Joe. If he tried to swerve out of the way, the movement would whip the open door back and forth, and Joe might lose his tenuous grasp.

Frank's only choice was to keep going straight ahead as fast as possible.

Joe's free hand stretched out, straining to

reach the top of the open door. His fingers clawed past the window glass and curled over the rim. Sliding his hand along the top of the door, he managed to pull himself close enough to swing one foot up onto the bumper. Grappling with the swaying door and inching his way closer, he finally got the other foot up. A few inches more and his feet were inside the van. But there wasn't much else he could do. His body was twisted and stretched at an awkward angle between the van and the open door. He didn't have the leverage or the footing to haul himself all the way in.

There was only one thing to do. "On the count of three," he screamed over the rushing wind, "hit the brakes! Got it?"

Frank understood immediately. "Got it!" he shouted back.

"One! Two! Three!" As the last word left his lips Joe dropped his hand from the rim of the door, hanging on with only one numb, tired hand.

In the same instant Frank tapped the brakes just hard enough to set Joe and the door moving in the right direction. Simple momentum carried Joe back into the van, and the door clanged shut behind him as he rolled toward the front of the van and bumped into the back of the passenger seat.

In the rearview mirror Frank could see the car closing in again, and he braced himself for another jarring impact. But at the last second the car veered into the left lane and darted past the van. For a few seconds before it sped off, Frank got a good look at the car and the rear license plate in the glow of the van's headlights.

Frank pulled over to the side of the road and helped his brother back into the front seat. Joe was slightly battered and dazed, and he fumbled with his seat belt for a few seconds before clicking it into the slot.

"Was it the black Jeep?" he asked hoarsely.

Frank nodded.

"Did you get the license number?"

Frank nodded again.

Joe gave his brother a quizzical look. "You don't seem too thrilled about it. I thought the whole idea was to draw him out in the open. I'd say we did a pretty good job of that. Now we can turn the license number over to the police, and they'll find out if Gemowski owns the Jeep."

"I doubt it," Frank responded. "The license plates were Canadian. They won't be easy to trace, and they were probably stolen anyway."

Joe slumped back in his seat. "Terrific. I almost got myself killed, and we have nothing to show for it. We don't know anything now that we didn't know before this disaster."

A slight grin crept over Frank's face. "Oh, I wouldn't say that. We know one thing we didn't know before."

Joe cast a sidelong glance at his brother. "What's that?"

141

"We know that you make one very ugly woman."

"That's it," Joe declared. "That's the last time I go along with one of your plans. From now on *I* make the plans."

"Go right ahead," Frank said. "Do you have any suggestions?"

"Lots of them," Joe claimed, racking his brain for a glimmer of an idea. "I just have to decide which one is best. I'll let you know when we get back to Vanessa's house."

"Here's my plan," Joe told Frank and Vanessa. "We're going to make a cartoon."

Frank stared at his brother. "We're going to *what?*"

"I think he said we're going to make a cartoon," Vanessa said.

"And then what?" Frank responded. "Make Gemowski watch it until he either laughs to death or confesses?"

"Good idea," Joe shot back. "If my plan doesn't work, we'll try that." He turned to Vanessa. "We'll need a couple of photographs. Do you have any pictures of the studio before the fire?"

"Sure," Vanessa said. "We took a whole bunch of shots before, during, and after the renovation of the barn."

"What about Phil Gemowski?" Joe asked. "Do you have any pictures of him?"

"Hold on," Vanessa replied. "Let me check." She went upstairs and came down with a stack of snapshots. "I took these at the big opening party Mom had in the studio," she explained. "Here's one of Phil—and here's another." She flipped through the pile and found several more pictures of Gemowski.

"So far, so good," Joe said. "Is there enough material here for you to make a realistic animated sequence of Gemowski alone in the studio?"

"That depends," Vanessa responded. "How realistic do you want it, and when do you need it?"

"Realistic enough to fool somebody for a little while," Joe told her. "And I need it tomorrow morning at the latest."

"I'll have to work all night!" Vanessa protested.

"We'll help," Joe said.

Joe described the action for the scene and then hovered over Vanessa's shoulder while she fed the photographs through the digital scanner and tinkered with the images on the computer. By ten o'clock she had a simple sequence of Gemowski walking across the screen. By midnight she had him moving around the studio, opening and closing doors.

"The movement looks pretty smooth and natural," Joe remarked. "but it looks flat, as if the figure was pasted onto the background or something."

"That's mostly a lighting problem," Vanessa explained. "The tricky part about putting an animated character and a real background together in a convincing manner is the way the light appears to fall on the character. When you walk across a room the light hits you from different angles. The shadows shift and change as you move. You may not normally be aware of it, but you notice when it's not there.

"I could add some shading," she continued, "but it'd take time, and I don't know if I'm a good enough artist to make it very realistic."

"There's an easier solution," Frank said, studying the image on the computer monitor. "Just make everything darker. I doubt he was sneaking around the studio with all the lights on, anyway. And even in good light, videotape comes out looking dark sometimes."

"That might work," Joe responded.

"And it's easy to do," Vanessa said. "Give me a few more minutes, and we should be ready to roll."

When they all agreed the scene was murky enough to hide the flaws without shrouding the identity of the star of the show, Vanessa slid a cassette into the video recorder next to the computer and hit the Record button.

"Here we go," she announced with a few final taps on the computer keyboard.

On the screen a shadowy figure entered the dim studio, crept over to the storage room, opened the door, and disappeared into the darkness. A minute or so later the figure came back out of the room and quickly left the studio.

When the short animated scene ended Vanessa

stopped the video recorder, rewound the tape, and played it back on the television. They watched it intently, rewound it, and played it again.

After the fifth replay Joe hit the Eject button and popped the cassette out of the machine. "It's almost perfect," he said. "Now for the final touch." He fished a pack of matches out of his coat pocket, lit one, and played it along the edges of the videocassette. The black plastic started to melt and smoke, sending a horrible stench into the air.

"Hey!" Vanessa cried out. "You'll ruin it!"

"I was just adding a few special effects," Joe said, blowing out the match. "The videotape was in a fire, remember?"

"Oh, right," Vanessa said. "So now that we have the tape, what do we do next?"

"Now I call Gemowski and tell him the news," Joe replied, picking up the telephone. He stared at the numbers for a moment and then smiled at Vanessa. "Did I ask you if you had his home phone number?"

Joe dialed the number Vanessa gave him and listened to the phone ring on the other end. After four rings there was a click, and a voice said, "Hi, this is Phil Gemowski. I can't come to the phone right now. Leave your message after the beep."

Joe waited for the electronic tone and then launched into the speech he had mentally prepared. "I guess you didn't know about the surveillance camera in the studio. I found the videocassette in the debris after the fire. It's a little crisp around the edges, but you can still play it. Most of it's pretty boring—but you have a really interesting walk-on scene.

"If you don't want the police to see it," he continued in a rough voice, "meet me at seven A.M. on the old access road in the woods behind the farm. You know where it is."

He hung up the phone and turned to his brother and Vanessa. "How did I sound?"

"Like a thug," Frank said. "You should be proud of yourself. Let's just hope it convinces Gemowski—and let's hope he has to use his Jeep to get through the deep snow on that access road."

At six forty-five the next morning Joe was hiding behind a tree in the woods, clutching a small portable television with a built-in videotape player. A few birds chirped away, oblivious to the cold, as the sun poked over the horizon, a large orange blob that didn't seem to give off any heat that day.

The distant rumble of a car engine grew closer, and Joe finally spotted the black Jeep coming down the road. The Jeep rolled to a stop in front of the small dead tree that had been dragged across the path. Joe waited for Gemowski to get out of the car before he showed himself.

"You're a little early," Joe said as he stepped out from behind the tree.

The man gave him a long, cold stare. "So are you," he said curtly. "What's this all about?"

Joe chuckled. "I think you know what this is about. You wouldn't be here if you didn't." He put the television on the hood of the Jeep and pressed the video Play button.

Gemowski stared at the tiny screen in silence.

"That's the original," Joe said when the tape was over. "There aren't any copies."

Gemowski looked at him. "Who else knows about this?"

"Nobody," Joe replied. "I figured it might be worth something, and I didn't want to split the profits with anybody. So I kept it to myself."

"Smart thinking," Gemowski said. "How much do you want for it?"

Joe put on a thin smile. "How much is it worth?"

Gemowski sighed and reached into his coat. "I'm afraid it's worth more than I could ever possibly pay you."

Joe froze as Gemowski's hand came out of the coat grasping a shiny snub-nosed revolver. He waved the gun in Joe's face and popped the videocassette out of the television. "I'm also afraid you know far too much," he said grimly, cocking the revolver and pointing it at Joe's forehead.

Chapter

17

JOE'S EYES LOCKED on Gemowski, deliberately ignoring the dark barrel of the gun. By itself the revolver was just a chunk of steel. The man holding it made it a deadly weapon. Joe could see doubt and hesitation in Gemowski's eyes. There was still a chance that Joe could talk his way out of this.

"You don't want to do that," he said with forced calm. "Another body is the last thing you need."

"You should have stayed out of it," Gemowski said. The revolver wavered slightly. "Nobody was supposed to get killed. I didn't know Skip was still in the studio. It was dark. I didn't see his car, and all the lights were off inside the studio. He must have been asleep in one of the offices."

148

"I know," Joe assured him. "It was an accident. That means you're not really a murderer—not yet, anyway. Turn yourself in, and maybe they'll go easy on you. But if you pull the trigger now, it's first-degree murder. You'll spend the rest of your life behind bars."

"Only if they catch me," Gemowski replied, bringing his other hand up to steady his gun arm.

"Oh, they'll catch you all right," Joe said quickly. "If *we* figured it out, how long do you think it will be before the police catch on?"

A troubled look crept over Gemowski's face. "We?" he echoed, letting the gun dip a few inches.

A shadow passed across Gemowski's face. He jerked his head back and swung the gun up. Joe's hand shot out, grabbing and twisting Gemowski's wrist as Frank dropped on the man from his hiding place in the overhanging branches.

The gun roared once, and Frank and Gemowski tumbled to the ground in a heap. Joe was still grappling with Gemowski's gun hand as he went down. Joe felt something snap in the man's arm. Gemowski howled with pain, dropping the gun and clutching his arm as he rolled in the snow.

Frank scooped up the gun and scrambled to his feet. He studied the revolver for a moment, flipped open the cylinder, and dumped out the bullets. He counted the shells and then held the gun up in the sunlight and squinted into the cylinder to make sure it was empty.

Joe grabbed the moaning man by his coat collar and hauled him up off the ground. "See what happens when you play with guns?" he said sternly, shaking his finger at Gemowski.

"My arm," Gemowski groaned. "I think you broke it."

"A broken arm is the least of your problems," Joe said.

"You can't prove that's me on that videotape," Gemowski retorted. "It may look a little like me, but it's too dark and blurry to tell for sure."

"That's okay," Frank said. "We have a much better one that you haven't seen yet." He looked up in to the tree branches. "Right?" he called out.

Vanessa smiled down from the tree, waving a video camera in the air. "Right!" she shouted back.

"Next time I'm hiring a stand-in to play my part," Joe said. "These action scenes can be hazardous to your health."

Frank and Joe hauled Gemowski into the police station and showed their videotape to the police chief. Soon after, Andrea Bender was out of jail. Chief Collig was more than happy to release her and lock up Phil Gemowski.

"You boys took a foolish risk," he lectured. "Next time you might not be so lucky. Police work isn't a game—it's dangerous business."

"Danger is my middle name," Joe said in his best tough-guy voice.

The police chief scowled and turned to Andrea. "You should have told us about Gemowski. We could have helped you."

"She didn't know it was Gemowski," Frank said.

Andrea looked at him. "How did you know that?"

Frank shrugged. "A logical deduction. Why would he identify himself? A faceless, unknown enemy is much more frightening and harder to fight than one you know."

"And you didn't have to know who he was to believe his phone threats," Joe added. "His actions were convincing enough. He wanted you to think he could kill Vanessa any time he wanted, and there was nothing you could do about it except play along and do exactly what he told you to do."

"He sure had me convinced," Andrea said. "And I guess I wasn't thinking very clearly. The 'accidents,' the threats on Vanessa's life, the fire, Skip's death, and the pressure of trying to meet the deadline for the show were all a little too much for me to handle."

"Do you really think Phil would have killed me if Mom hadn't confessed?" Vanessa asked.

Frank shook his head. "No. He didn't set out to kill anybody in the first place. Skip Guzman was just in the wrong place at the wrong time.

I don't know if he could have made himself pull the trigger on Joe this morning."

"And I'm glad you didn't wait to find out," Joe said.

"What about the gas explosion at Lynn St. Pierre's house?" Chief Collig responded. "Wasn't he trying to kill her?"

"Think about it," Frank said. "If Lynn dies, the whole writing team for the show is gone. Then Gemowski would have to find somebody else to write it. Maybe he would find somebody who could do a good job, and maybe he wouldn't— but why take the risk?"

The police chief frowned. "You tell me," he said gruffly.

"It's pretty obvious," Frank said. "It was a red herring that got out of control."

"A red herring?" Andrea echoed, a puzzled look on her face.

"A diversion," Frank explained. "Gemowski wanted us to think that somebody wanted to kill the show completely."

"Somebody like Bert Zall?" Vanessa ventured.

"Exactly," Joe said. "Gemowski never expected the gas leak to demolish the house. He just wanted everybody to think somebody wanted to get rid of both of 'Rex Rover's' creators."

"And when that didn't work," Frank said, "he stepped up his staged attacks on Vanessa."

"Stepped up?" Vanessa echoed. "Do you mean there were other attacks that I didn't know about?"

"You knew about them," Frank replied. "You just didn't know they were directed at you. Remember the day we met you? Somebody had slashed all the tires on your car."

"At the time we figured they got your car by mistake," Joe said, picking up the story. "But it was no mistake. Gemowski probably hoped that a lot of little 'accidents' like that might be enough to make you guys pack up and leave town, leaving 'Rex Rover' unfinished."

"Then there was the rock that hit the van's windshield," he continued.

"Wait a second," Vanessa cut in. "How did he know I was in your van? And don't tell me he followed us, because he couldn't have been on top of the viaduct and in a car behind us at the same time."

"That had me stumped for a while, too," Frank said. "Then I remembered two important facts. First, the viaduct goes over the only road that leads to your house. Second, Gemowski knew we had given you a ride to school in the van. He was at your house that morning, so he knew there was a good chance we'd give you a ride home, too. All he had to do was get into position and wait."

"Well, he'll be doing his waiting in a jail cell from now on," the police chief said. "Phil Gemowski will be behind bars for a long time."

"Just think of all the episodes of 'Rex Rover' he'll miss," Andrea said.

"Does that mean you still have a chance to finish the show on time?" Frank asked.

Andrea smiled and put her arm around Vanessa. "Nothing can stop us now."

Joe looked at Vanessa. "I guess that means you'll be in town for a while."

"That's right," Vanessa said. "But I'll probably be busy most of the time."

Joe stared down at his feet. "Oh, sure. I understand."

"After I help my mom get back on schedule with 'Rex Rover,' " Vanessa explained, "I have my own animated show to work on."

Joe glanced up and saw the impish grin on her face. "You don't mean—"

Vanessa nodded. "The cartoon adventures of Joe Hardy."

Frank laughed. "I can't wait to see it—but I don't think it will ever be very popular."

"You're just jealous," Joe said.

Frank slapped his brother on the back. "No, that's not it. I just don't think any cartoon could ever be nearly as funny as your real-life antics."

Frank and Joe's next case:

The Hardy boys are bound on a perilous troubleshooting mission. Destination: the Deep Six, a floating oil rig in the Gulf of Mexico. The brothers have gone undercover—Frank as a helicopter pilot, Joe as a jack-of-all-trades—to find out who's trying to destroy the operation, putting four giant rigs and their crews at risk.

The Hardys learn that an eco-terrorist organization is openly opposed to the rigs. But they also find that bad blood in this business flows as thick as the oil, and that the truth may be as treacherous as a tropical storm. They've landed in the middle of a high-seas battleground—a dirty war that could trigger ecological disaster at any moment . . . in *Rigged for Revenge*, Case #70 in The Hardy Boys Casefiles™.